Tim MacGabhann was born in Kilkenny, Ireland, and began his writing career as a music journalist while studying English Literature and French at Trinity College, Dublin. Since 2013, he has reported from all over Latin America for outlets including *Esquire* and the *Washington Post*. His fiction and non-fiction appears in the *Dublin Review* and the *Stinging Fly*, and he holds an M.A. in Creative Writing from the University of East Anglia. He is the author of the critically acclaimed novel *Call Him Mine*, which was selected by the *Daily Telegraph* as one of their 'Thrillers of the Year'. He lives in Mexico City.

·HOW·TO·BE·
NOWHERE

TIM MACGABHANN

WEIDENFELD & NICOLSON

First published in Great Britain in 2020 by Weidenfeld & Nicolson
This paperback edition published in Great Britain in 2021
by Weidenfeld & Nicolson
an imprint of The Orion Publishing Group Ltd
Carmelite House, 50 Victoria Embankment
London EC4Y 0DZ

An Hachette UK Company

1 3 5 7 9 10 8 6 4 2

Copyright © Tim MacGabhann 2020

A CIP catalogue record for this book is
available from the British Library.

ISBN (Paperback) 978 1 4746 1050 6
ISBN (eBook) 978 1 4746 1051 3

Typeset by Input Data Services Ltd, Somerset

Printed and bound in Great Britain by Clays Ltd, Elcograf S.p.A.

www.orionbooks.co.uk
www.weidenfeldandnicolson.co.uk

'The Prince of Darkness is a gentleman,
Modo he's called, and Mahu.'

– William Shakespeare, *King Lear*, Act 3, Sc. iv

'The sea was wet as wet could be,
The sands were dry as dry.
You could not see a cloud, because
No cloud was in the sky:
No birds were flying overhead –
There were no birds to fly.

The Walrus and the Carpenter
Were walking close at hand;
They wept like anything to see
Such quantities of sand.'

– Lewis Carroll, 'The Walrus and the Carpenter',
from *Through the Looking-Glass*

I

On the morning that the phone calls started, I dreamed that Carlos and I were back in Poza Rica, back in that place where nobody had asked us to go, back where nobody had asked us to look. This was where my mind lived at night – in a bar with riveted portholes for windows, a slow ocean of fog breaking against the panes, the river slopping black against the glass leaving a thick drag of foam. An oil derrick clanked behind the bar, pumping stout into a pyramid of glasses, while the dead kid we'd found, Julián Gallardo, lay on the bar at the centre of an altar we had made around him.

It's like I told you before: nobody had asked Carlos and I to look at that body. But we had, and then everything had fallen apart. Julián had been an activist, murdered by corrupt local police. We'd never known him when he'd been alive, never even met him, but nobody had changed my life more. Carlos and I had found him lying dead and faceless at the bottom of an alley, and only I had lived to tell the tale.

There's no need to tell you how big a news story that had been. That story was the reason I'd had to leave Mexico.

Two shots, the forensics technician had told me, outside the apartment where Carlos had died, *the first between third and fourth rib on the right side, fatally puncturing a lung.*

In the dream Carlos stepped up beside me. Smoke crinkled out of the bullet-holes in his chest.

'Jesus' – his fingernail clinked against my glass – 'of all the ways to crack, you pick *Carlsberg*? No mames, vato.'

Three years since my last drink or line, six months since I'd gone around dosing my grief with swigs of diluted LSD from a dinged metal water flask, and yet here I was, a pint in my hand, saying, 'Hey, come on, man, it's a premium lager.'

'Doesn't taste like it, vato.' He lifted the pint and took a deep gulp. Something hissed wetly inside him as he swallowed.

The second shot between fifth and sixth rib on the left side, destroying the heart completely.

Carlos tucked his shirt back in and leaned forward to reach for one of the glasses in the pyramid. A poppy collar of bruises ringed his neck. In the creamy whorls of reds and browns I saw oil, blood, smoke.

A reverse chokehold fractured the hyoid bone.

'Try this instead, vato,' he said, and held the glass out to me. His vibe was different from before, stand-offish, cold, like those white marble statues of Ancient Greece, of Orpheus or Eurydice or someone, I don't know. 'It'll kill you. But gently, you know?'

The fizz spritzed my face like drizzle.

'It could all be over if you just let yourself drown, vato,' Carlos said. His voice was gentle, his fingers were broken, and his eyes were pinkish with petechial haemorrhaging.

Three years.

Six months.

But now my mouth was dripping with the thirst, and my throat became a long ache. A sob rose and fell in my chest. My hand was lifting the glass all by itself.

Then gravel crunched. A siren cut through my skull. Police-car lights washed over Carlos and me and Julián Gallardo, red and blue and halogen white, and Carlos' killer – half his head missing, his police-uniform stained – stepped out of the light.

2

My eyes opened. Maya's knuckles were rapping the car window.

'You said you'd be at Arrivals!' she said and swung open the door.

'And where did I park?' I swallowed the cobwebs in my mouth, pointed at the red sign glowing above the airport door. It was a foggy night. There weren't many cars.

'As in, *standing* at Arrivals.' She slung her bag into the back seat and sat in the front.

'Ah, no, that was a bridge too far.' I yawned and started the car. Coffee cups and donut boxes rattled at my feet. But, as I was about to turn around, I saw a white face standing beside a jeep, a white face wearing wraparound sunglasses and a square beard.

'You going to drive or what?' Maya said.

'Huh?' I blinked. The face vanished. It could have been anything – frames from a dream, a flash of bad memory, whatever, I saw stuff that wasn't there all the time these days. 'Oh. Yeah.'

'You spaced out there,' Maya said.

'Occupational hazard.' I drove us away from the airport, turned us onto the highway from Montevideo back to Colonia.

'What occupation?' Maya said. 'You haven't been doing shit since you moved here.'

'I don't know, managing trauma, or whatever. Speaking of which: you ready to talk yet?'

'Not really, no.' She reached into the back seat, rummaged for a second, then pulled out a giant orange candle shaped like an elephant.

'We're good for candles,' I said, and then I saw the needle as thick as my finger that was stuck in the elephant's flank, and the note – '*GET OUT OF HERE, WHORE*' – that the needle was holding in place.

'Oh, right,' I said.

'This was in my hotel room,' she said. 'In Poza Rica.'

You remember all this – Maya had been due to stay with us while she did the write-up of the investigation into what Carlos and I had uncovered in Veracruz, all about how the state government and oil companies had been using gang members and bad cops as death squads to drive indigenous people off their land, to silence activists, and to threaten journalists into silence. The governor and his people would launder their money by paying companies that didn't exist for public services that wouldn't happen.

After all that stuff had come to light, it had seemed a lot safer to dig around, and so that's what Maya had been doing. Yeah, well, there's safe, and there's Mexican safe.

Meaning Maya's editor had called you and I the night before, saying he'd paid to change her flight, and would be sending her down on the first plane that could get her to us.

'Any idea why?' I said. The road's broken white dividing line flicked towards me through the dark. My heartbeat was starting to quicken.

'Those shell companies.' Maya eased her seat back with a click. 'I went to their addresses – you know, all these fake places. Taxi-ranks. Old peoples' homes. Oxxos. Last one I went to was in an open-air car park. Guy was sitting there, this old guy, a few curls of hair left. And so I ask him, "Are you the CEO of this company?", and I hold up the piece of paper I had printed out from the Freedom of Information request, and he spits and says, "I look like one for you", which sounds like a fucking "Yes" to me, quite frankly, but whatever, I go back to the hotel, and the manager's at reception, and he waves me over, and he lifts this candle out from behind the desk, and this enormous valet comes up behind me with my bags. Y ya.' She did jazz-hands at me. 'So here I am.'

'Thought you didn't want to talk.'

'Nature finds a way,' she said, easing back against the seat.

'That's terrifying, though. Jesus.'

'Occupational hazard. How're you, anyway?'

'Oh, you know. Happy. Quietly so. But happy.'

Maya looked at me sidelong. I could never get anything past her.

'Is that code for "bored"?' she said.

'No comment.' I flipped the indicator. 'It's just new, you know?'

'I'm still hearing "bored".'

'"Bored" is good,' I said. '"Bored" means safe. I *wish* I was bored. But I'm still too scared.' The roadside lamps striped the inside of the car with white light. 'Yeah,' said Maya, staring out at the dark. 'I hear you.'

'Could do with all of that stuff being ten years ago already. Like a dog snapping at my heels.'

Maya didn't say anything.

I pointed at the elephant. The needle was stuck fast in a divot of wax. 'They let you fly with that thing?'

'Told them it was an art project.'

'Fair.'

The night was clear, quiet – no light pollution blotting at the glitter of the stars, no chug and thud of cumbia from the clubs, no kids trying to sell us knock-off Marlboro Red at the lights. It was basically the opposite of Mexico City around here. Sometimes I hated that.

'You hungry or anything?' I asked, as we slowed towards the Old Town. The orb lamps on the main square made me feel like I was back in Mexico City's half-wrecked Centro Histórico backstreets. The nick of woodsmoke on the air briefly became the tang of beer-suds, the just-fucked musk and rained-on leather of the clubs became mine and Carlos' sweat-run aftershave, but I shoved the memory away.

'Not really, no,' said Maya. 'Wouldn't say no to a cheeky cigarette though, yeah?'

'Get thee behind me, Satan.'

She nodded off not long after that. Shock'll do that to you. The sallow bones of a right whale glowed in a display sunk

7

into the wall of the fortress, and I turned past it and slowed towards home. Maya woke at the snapping-bone noise of the brake.

'Wow,' she said when she saw the house. 'Nice place.'

'Ah yeah,' I said, and got out to carry her bags. Inside I got her settled in the spare room downstairs.

'Right so,' I said, and gave her a hug. 'Sleep well.'

'If I can,' she said.

'I believe in you,' I said. 'You need anything, just scream.'

'Blood-curdling or standard?'

'Oh, standard will do.' I shut the door and climbed up the stairs.

3

'Those are getting really bad,' you said, at the sound of me coming into the room.

'What are?' I sat down on the edge of the bed and took off my shoes.

'Those nightmares of yours,' you said.

My hand stopped in mid-air. 'You mean I had another one?' I said. 'Huh. Can't even remember it.'

'You should see someone,' you said.

'What, like an affair?' I lay down. 'There'll be no poly-amory in this house.'

'Like a *therapist*.' You swatted me with the back of your hand. 'You're still seeing him, aren't you?' You'd been good about the Carlos dreams at the start. But it's hard to stay patient with someone who's just not getting better, I suppose.

You checked the time on your phone, then flopped back down again. 'Oh, for God's sake.' You folded the pillow around your head with one arm. Your Peñarol jersey had ridden up, so I smoothed it down to cover your back, but you jerked away. 'Your fingers are freezing!'

'Alright, alright.' I swung my legs from the bed to pull on my track-pants.

Your alarm went off. You flailed, batted the mattress with your fist.

'Let me get that.' I reached under your pillow, found the phone, pressed *Snooze*, then zipped up my hoodie.

'How is she?' you said.

'Yeah, OK. And excited to meet you. I've been bragging.'

'Liar.'

Bluish 5 a.m. light threw the shadows of firs against the blinds of your bedroom. The dodgy floorboard creaked as I laid my foot down.

'How did you wind up upside-down?' I rubbed your chest.

'Your bad dream. You yelped.' You wiggled a little, scratching yourself. 'Thought it was the alarm. So I sat up. But then I fell back asleep.' You yawned and stretched, kicking, then squeaked like those otters whose Instagram you followed. 'And then I fell over. Now quiet.' You pulled my pillow over your head. 'Too early for speech.'

A plump cinnamon blur zipped past the glass, cheeping insistently, as I climbed down the ladder from the loft room.

'Alright, alright,' I said. 'I'm coming.'

After shoving nuts into the plastic feeder by the door, I went downstairs to light the stove. Maya was sitting at the kitchen table, her laptop open.

'What, no sleep?'

'Too wired.' Her chin rested on both her hands. 'There's coffee.'

'Nice one.' I heated water for your yerba maté and turned my phone on.

A missed call popped up from a Mexico City number and the breath went steam-hot in my nose.

'What?' Maya said.

She looked at me.

Like I said – there was nothing I could ever get past her. My knuckles rapped the table.

'Anyone after you?' I said. 'Like, specifically.'

'That I know of?' She shook her head.

'Nobody who'd, like, follow you here. For example.'

'Don't think so.'

'Alright.' I held up the phone. 'Like, I could be just being paranoid. But I got a wrong-number call, and, well. I don't know.' I blocked the number. 'Maybe it's nothing.'

Maya looked at me over the rim of her mug.

'Shit.'

I started doing my stretches – hand against the wall, leg raised, everything like that. 'It'd be worse if you weren't here.'

Maya bobbed her head from side to side.

'I mean, for me, maybe.'

The kettle boiled, and I stopped stretching to fill your Thermos and to tamp yerba into your favourite maté gourd. The rumble of the boiler and the slap of sud-thickened water were filtering down from upstairs.

'Don't think about it.' I lifted the Thermos and gourd. 'Just going to feed the kraken now.' I went upstairs.

★

'Maya OK?' you said, from inside the shower, when you heard me come through the door.

'Ah, yeah.'

I opened the door and held the straw through the gap so you could sip while you shampooed yourself.

'Maybe you should ask her how she's dealing with all the stuff she's got going on.' You turned away from me, into the spray.

'What stuff?'

'I don't know. The stories she does. They're a bit like yours.'

'Yeah. Maybe.'

The anger surged through me, then the shame. All you knew of the story was what everybody knew – that Carlos' killer was dead, and so was the owner of the company responsible for all the horror we'd uncovered, a man called Roberto Zúñiga. What you didn't know was that I'd been there on the night that Zúñiga had been shot, and that I'd been sent there by his killers as a diversion tactic.

The wrong number I'd seen on the screen of my phone flashed in my head, my chest went tight again, and I sat down on the toilet, huffing as much as I could of your menthol shampoo, your Carolina Herrera 212 body-wash, your pH-neutral face-soap, into my lungs.

'Is she seeing anyone?' you asked after a minute or so.

'Like dating?' I said, even though I knew where this was going.

'Andrew.'

'Right. I'll ask.' I left the gourd beside the sink and opened the door and leant in to give you a kiss on the back of your neck. There was no point saying anything else, and that's not because we were speaking Spanish: it'd be hard in any language, because there are things you can see, and there are things that happen to you, and there are things you can talk about, and they're really never the same set of things. 'Back in a bit.'

'OK,' you said. 'Love you too.'

Maya had gone back to her room when I got downstairs. Outside, I left my hood down so the drizzle could freshen me awake. The tang of rain on fallen pine-needles gave me a shiver. My breath smoked in the air. All of that was more real than the dreams, I tried to tell myself, but none of it was more real than the stuff that was still following Maya and me around.

The firs were a thin black cursive against the white fog. Red-bibbed degollados were hopping around the ruined fortress, and the sky was fishbelly-grey, with thunderheads massing in the east. The air stank, though, a dog-food odour of rotting sargassum weed. For weeks now, brown clumps of the stuff had been coming in with the tide, killing the beach-wedding industry. Some papers said that an algal bloom had fed the weed. Other papers said that the algae had only bloomed because the sea was up half a degree from this time a year ago.

'Guess you just warmed this place right up,' you had said one morning, kicking a clump of the stuff as we walked along the strand. 'My warm-hearted European.'

'That's not the stereotype at all,' I'd replied, but you just laughed. Today a small yellow digger was clearing a track through the heaps of seaweed that covered the place we'd been walking that day.

A chunk of wall loomed up to one side of me as I ran, the words UNIVERSO PARALELO ENTRADA AQUÍ beginning to fade from the whitewash. The black dog who lived on the beach sprang from his tussock of grass and jogged over to rub himself along my trailing hand.

'Buenos días, güey,' I said.

He warbled, tossed his head so hard that dirt and gravel flew from his moustache, then began to run alongside me. Drifts of mist cooled my shins and darkened the hairs on his legs. Razor-shells and pebbles crunched underfoot, and I hopped a sea-darkened plank of wood, dodged a vodka bottle sunk past its neck in sand. A gull squawked at me from a nest of toothbrushes, clothes-pegs, and old combs, her head blotched and her eyes reddened by whatever was in the sea that morning.

'So much for her,' I said to the dog. 'How're you getting on?'

He just panted.

'Yeah.' I was starting to pant as well. 'I feel you.'

The Mar del Plata was a grey shimmer that slowly ignited to white as I ran. When my watch beeped a count of ten thousand steps, I let myself drop onto the sand, my eyes shut, my legs shaking, my breath a raw scorch, too tired to be scared any more. Moments like that, they're what I used to drink for, that emptied-out clarity, where all you are is what's happening around you – the salt nick of the air, the cool sand under your nape, the crash of the ocean loud and rhythmic and pouring into your ears.

The dog stood over me, his tail beating the strand.

'Mind these, won't you?' I stripped off my T-shirt and shorts and stepped out of my shoes.

The dog sneezed.

I launched myself into waves gone reddish with leaf-shred. Tapes of sargassum wrapped around my shins. Six waves out, the water was so cold that it felt like a scald. When I was done swimming, I let the tide drag me shorewards.

'Much appreciated,' I said to the dog as I retrieved my things.

He didn't pay much attention: that fat brown Labrador, the one who slept in your hotel's driveway, she'd showed up to sniff him, and he was trying to play it cool.

The café had opened. After getting a three-chili brownie and a flat white to go, I headed past the pier, and another flash hit me from the previous night's dream – a boat slowing towards the dock, a man with a scar down the middle of his face chucking a mooring rope, Carlos' corpse pulling the blanket from his face – and I had to close my eyes, lean my forehead against a wall, wait the pictures out.

A tinny whirr lowered in behind me, and I turned, saw the lens of a small white drone glinting back at me, the red dot of its recorder beady, red, insect-like.

For a second it was hard to tell whether the drone was really there or not, and I just stood there gawping in my shorts, with a coffee in my hand, while the drone yawed off towards the fortress.

A vein ticked in my temple. The coffee was lukewarm by the time my legs felt steady enough to walk home.

That's how it is, this reporting thing.

Sometimes you find out the truth.

Sometimes the truth finds out where you live.

4

A tallow fog had settled in, leaving nothing visible below my knees. My breath smoked in the cold, and a metal tang of fallen leaves cut my nose, light slicing the mist above the screen of poplars around our garden. After the drone, after the flashes of the dream, I wished those trees had been a wall topped with broken glass instead.

Inside, you'd left a Post-It on the kitchen table, sketched with a heart ('*For the tea*,' you'd written) and a middle finger ('*For the wake-up*'). Maya was standing in the middle of the kitchen floor, worrying her lip with her teeth, a coffee cup steaming in her grip.

'What happened?' I dabbed the sweat from my forehead with one of your old SlimFast facecloths.

'You're not going to like it,' she said, and pointed to her laptop, which sat on the low maple table by the couch.

A story from the *Guardian* was open on the screen. The headline read '*Veracruz governor flees to Guatemala as lawyer fights assets freeze*', and I felt myself dry up and scatter like styrofoam pebbles across the tiles. I saw my hand swing up, flinging my coffee against the ground, and heard the rattle of the cup against the floor, but I couldn't feel myself doing it.

'Fuck,' I managed to say. 'I just.' I swallowed. 'I was really looking forward to that trial.'

'You and all of Veracruz.'

'Yeah, well, you know what I mean.' I crossed the room to fetch some paper towels, then knelt to the creamy brown spill, attacking the grouting before it could stain. 'They keep getting away with it. These rich fucks.'

'Zúñiga didn't get away with it,' Maya said.

'One isn't enough.' I flopped onto the couch.

'True,' she said. 'Plus, you know, the governor, he's the one who made it all happen – the deals with the companies, the deals with the gangs.'

'All that shit,' I said. My voice was tight. I was thinking of Carlos, of the morning I'd watched the paramedics carry his body down the stairs, of his brown hair overhanging the red blanket, each wave of it stiff with blood. 'It'll never come out in court now.'

'There's no court hard enough for that kind of thing.' She put her hands over her face, massaging her forehead with her fingertips. 'This is going to be so bad for my book. Does that sound bad?'

'Not at all.' I carried the cup to the sink. The thing was crumpled, I'd thrown it so hard. I sat down on the couch again. 'Let's have a proper gawk, shall we?'

'You'll get an ulcer,' Maya said, a warning arch in her voice, but she sat down beside me anyway.

The article's top picture was of the governor himself, Janiel Uruchurtu, adjusting his tortoiseshell Burberry specs as he stood before a mic'd-up podium.

'I covered that press conference,' Maya said. 'After another journalist got killed. It's the one where he said "If you keep quiet, nobody will get crucified". Just grinning at the press pool, yeah? Like a shark.'

'Fucker.'

The next photo is the governor's lawyer jogging up the steps of the Procuraduría General's office, an iPhone at her ear, her hair auburn, coiffed, enormous.

'God, I even hate his lawyer,' I said. 'Anytime I wear that much black, all you can see is dandruff.'

'They really go to town on the governor,' Maya said, flicking down through the text. 'An account of his wine-cellar.'

'Fifteenth-century Lebanese vintages,' I read. 'Jesus. A million dollars.'

'They left out his sandwich helicopter, though.'

'What's that?'

'Oh, he kept sending it to collect tortas from, like, this tiny roadside puesto. The helicopter literally wore out, yeah? Crashed and killed the pilot.'

'I suppose that's one way of bankrupting a state.'

'Literally.'

The third photo showed where all the money had come from: a six-year-old girl in a hospital bed, the frame holed with rust, the sheets coffee-coloured with dirt, the saline drip in her arm patched up with a Band-Aid.

'That's a photo of the cancer hospital,' Maya said, tapping the screen. 'They said they were giving kids state-of-the-art chemo treatments, but it was just saltwater.' She shook her head. 'Fuck, I mean, nobody ever pays for this.'

More photos followed: Uruchurtu and his wife and his mistress at their executive box in the Bernabéu stadium; their collection of Matisses and Boteros and Picassos; his Oxford student son decked out in full Bullingdon-Club regalia; their lush ranches in Texas, Chiapas, Guatemala. The last one caught my eye, an English-style mansion complete with mansard roof in a foggy highland nowhere. La Faena, it was called, according to the caption. Fog streaked the front of the stonework, dripping from the eaves.

'A whole lot of bodies paid for that house,' Maya said, then moved on. She stopped at a photo of the Torre 1521, '*the unofficial security headquarters of the whole administration.*'

'This is one of the places I went,' she said, tapping the screen, which showed a fifteen-storey prow of steel and glass built by one of the governor's pals, looking right out at the dirt-coloured sea beyond Boca del Río, the windows sepia with pollution. A bald lot was on one side, and a half-wrecked fairground on the other, where Goofy, Mickey Mouse, and The Beatles shed their paintwork to the sea air.

'He had all these right-wing nerds working there,' Maya said. 'They'd been setting up whole armies of Twitter bots to threaten activists. They'd publish this clickbait, yeah? About Communist activists turning militant, and stealing oil, or whatever, but they'd touch up these old '90s photos of Zapatistas as, like "proof".'

In my head I could see all the things that I'd seen in Veracruz, all the horrors Uruchurtu's money and power had made happen, and I was there again, outside Poza Rica, with an indigenous Totonaca couple I'd interviewed, Tomás and Apolonia, and their house surrounded by poisoned banana-leaves, a smell of petrol rising from their well, telling me about the Zeta gang members dressed as police who'd tried to scare them off their land.

'That tower's where Uruchurtu's cops would send the drones from.' The text of the article scrolled down Maya's glasses, flipped around as if in a mirror. 'One-point-six-million megapixel cameras flying over activists' houses.'

In my head I saw Carlos kneeling above the kid we'd found, saw an ant picking across the wet red mask of his face.

'Plus the jeeps, and the police cars, roaring around the town,' Maya went on. 'Signal-jammers to silence protests – these little blue boxes that you can put on a car-bonnet. Phone-tapping stuff from Israel.'

In my head I saw Carlos and me on our knees in the white glare of the police lights, hands above our heads, glass pricking my knees through my jeans.

'You don't happen to have any smokes, do you?'

'For you?' Maya looked at me sidelong, her mouth a crease. 'No.'

'Alright, alright.' I leaned my head against the couch and let a groan leak out of my mouth. 'Forced to bare-back real-ity, once again.'

Maya rubbed her eyes. 'I'm so fucking tired.'

The front door opened. You appeared in the doorway. Maya and I both jumped.

'Wow,' you said. 'It's only me, c'mon.' You were holding paper bags. 'Do I need to worry?'

'No!' I said, too fast.

Maya punched the couch for emphasis. 'Absolutely not!'

You looked back and forth between us. 'That's extremely reassuring.' You saw the mess of kitchen towels on the floor, you laid the bags down on the table and kneeled to pick the towels up.

'Ah, crap,' I said. 'Sorry. That was me.'

'Oh, I know,' you said. 'Maya, was he always like this?'

'Worse, if anything,' Maya said.

'You two met, what, an hour ago?' I said. 'And already you're ganging up on me?'

'Yes,' you said.

'A hundred per cent,' said Maya.

'Oh, whatever. Here, let me bin those,' I said. 'Let me cleanse my shame off.'

'Nah. I've got it.' You pitched the wad of papers overarm. It bounced against the cupboard door, dropped through the flap of the inorganic waste bin.

'Three points,' I said. My body was tense all over from the news, but just to see you come through the door, from that normal world you helped me pretend we were living in – I don't know, it sent relief rinsing down through me.

'Nice you're home early,' Maya said.

'Yeah, I haven't got anyone staying today. Even the restaurant's super quiet – think the seaweed effect is beginning to hit.'

'Uh oh,' Maya said.

'No, no, it's good. I'm exhausted.' You eased down onto my lap. '"*Embezzled billions*",' you read from the screen. 'God.'

'Don't read it,' said Maya. 'It's too depressing.'

You scrolled back up.

'Oh, but this is your guy,' you said. 'The big boss.' You got to the top, saw the headline. 'Oh. Oh no.'

'Yeah, well, what can you do?' I pressed a hand to your back, moving you off my lap and away from the laptop. A police photo was beaming out from the point in the article where you'd scrolled back up to, one that showed a man with a scar running down the centre of a face I'd last seen in the front seat of a Veracruz State Police car, telling me when and where to be on the night he planned to kill Roberto Zúñiga, his eyes lasering two spots of heat into my back as Maya and I followed you over to the kitchen counter.

5

To go with the food you'd brought from the hotel, Maya and I pressed and deep-fried some quesadillas, filled with the potato and green pepper mix I'd made the day before. After eating, you sat back in the chair beside mine with a satisfied groan, patting your stomach.

'Oh, wow,' you said. 'And you can get these everywhere in Mexico?'

'Pretty much every second block of every city,' Maya said.

'They're far better than this, though,' I said, looking at the fried curl of dough between my fingers.

'So you *do* miss Mexico.' You spooned up a little salsa and tasted it from the end of your finger. 'Wow. Hot, though.'

'Oh, that's just a mild version,' Maya said.

'The chilis here are for babies,' I said. 'Impossible to get a good one.'

'We do our best,' you said, a little defensively.

'Chimichurri doesn't count,' Maya said.

'Chimichurri's from *Argentina*.' You pointed at me. 'That's like confusing England and Ireland for him.'

'Oh, but he loves that,' Maya said.

The curl of fried dough between my fingers had come out golden-brown and crispy. It reminded me less of food-stalls than it did of a video I'd once seen, at a soldier's house somewhere outside Acapulco. Half-way through the video, a brownish shard of someone's vertebra had struck the camera.

You swooped in to collect my plate.

'Ah, thank you. Sorry, just reminiscing.' I swabbed the end of the quesadilla through a stain of salsa roja as you lifted away the plate. 'Heavily.'

'It's that story about the governor, isn't it?' you said.

'Love, you don't need to worry,' I said, as that Mexico City number flashed in my head again, the number and the drone.

'Yeah, why would you?' Maya said. 'You're not the one writing a book about it.'

'Well, you both seem to know an awful lot about it. And you're both here.' You were running water.

'We're just voyeurs.' I tipped the salsa into a plastic tupper-ware and clicked shut the lid.

The cordless home phone shrilled from its cradle beside the table.

'Andrew, could you get that?'

'Yep.' I crossed the room, lifted the phone and put it back without lifting the receiver to my ear. You gave me a sour look.

'What?'

'That was rude.'

'To who?'

'To me. Someone's trying to call my house and you hang up on them?' You clanked a plate onto the drying-rack.

Maya was looking around the room, trying to find an excuse to get out of there, but then her own phone rang and rescued her.

'Ah, fuck.' She looked at the screen, where her editor's name was flashing. 'Right, back in a bit,' she said, then scooped up her laptop and went into her room, shutting the door behind her.

'You really need to see someone.' Another plate clanked onto the rack. 'This is paranoia. Pure and simple.'

'Yeah. Maybe.' I scratched my neck. Photos from that year you spent at sea hung on the walls of the room I was in – the lighted galleries of a passenger ferry near Bermuda; a helicopter's shadow racing over waves; shoreline pyramids and a violet dawn somewhere in Southeast Asia; a legion of Portuguese Man-o'-War, the fins gelid and electric purple, the entrail-coils of their tentacles dragging behind for half a mile or more. I saw the whole room trashed and destroyed, just like my apartment back in Mexico City – your maple table, your neat black lampshades, your photos from your big sailing trip pristine in their frames, I saw photos, all of that toppled, all of that ruined – the fridge tipped over, my failed salsas dribbled across the tiles, clots of broken glass on the stones of the Nikken water-filter, 'Z' for Zeta slashed into the couch. My chest felt tight and hot. I had about two hours until my Narcotics Anonymous meeting, but you didn't even know what day they were on, let alone what time. I took out my car keys and let them spin in circles from the end of my finger.

'You just going to stand there?' You took the tea-towel from the handle of the oven door and waved it at me. 'Come on, there's loads to dry.'

'Ah I think I'll go out, actually.' Carlos' Fidel Castro key-ring whipped around and around. 'And talk to someone, you know?'

You dropped the towel and turned around. 'Fine.'

I went to the car and slid on Carlos' jacket, the sleeves still bandy-armed from the memory of his shape. Death has a dozen different smells: Carlos' was oxter-sweat, Armani Code, stale Delicados – a ghost trapped in the folds.

6

The car looked fucking stupid – a '98 Subaru Impreza, picked up on the cheap from Sancho, an agronomist who'd learned his English from *Deep Space Nine* and Xbox Live, and who was tonight's chair at my Narcotics Anonymous group – with its double red stripe travelling bumper to bumper, leather seats that Sancho had told me, in a voice as grave as Picard's, had 'cost the lives of six Argentine steer'. But I loved it anyway, especially that subwoofer, the one that shot little puffs of air against the sides of my calves whenever I put the volume all the way up.

The glove compartment had a good lock on it, too, which was useful – I kept all the things there that I didn't want you to find, all the things that reminded me of Carlos, of Mexico, of everything I'd never be able to get back.

For a while I just drove around until my head was more or less quiet, zipping around the ring roads, past the blur of the petrol-station forecourts and the blue-lit diners and those little Alpine-lodge restaurants stationed beyond the treeline, memories of Carlos scattered on the passenger seat, playing in my head. On top lay the printed-out photo of the kid Carlos and I had found, his face a skinless mask, his teeth bared in a grimace of pain without end. That photo lay beside the copy of *Proceso* that had Carlos' face on the cover, and beside that was an acid blotter printed onto the face of Gustavo Díaz Ordáz, who'd been president at the time of the 1968 Tlatelolco Massacre. Carlos and I had bought it on his first day in Mexico City, after he'd moved down from El Paso. In my hands was the cardboard envelope of Carlos' ashes, given to me by his mother. The first time he and I had met, he'd talked about wanting to move to this very town, because he'd visited here with his mother when he'd been a teenager. He'd daydreamed aloud about shredding his photos into the surf, forgetting everything he'd seen, everything he'd photographed, everything that had destroyed him. Maybe he'd have preferred me to scatter his ashes here, but the thought of his last atoms greying the waves, darkening some random rock-chunk off Antarctica, it froze me up too much to do anything but keep him with me, so we could both live out his dream of a quiet life far from all the murder.

My knuckles rapped the envelope, and my mind went back to the day when me and Carlos had bought the acid, on his first Saturday in Mexico City. All afternoon, we'd smoked our brains out on the UNAM campus, bought sushi en route to mine, and we stopped to look at my favourite mural – the one that decorated the front of the Teatro de los Insurgentes, the one that was all smoke and fumes and scarlet drapes twisting above a cast of yelling revolutionaries and indigenous

29

men, women glammed up like European duchesses – the one that I'd seen in my grandfather's house in Bagenalstown, the one that I'd spent my whole life waiting to stand in front of, the one that I'd lived two blocks away from when I'd first moved here, the one that I'd been so desperate to show him, lit up white against the blue evening. Carlos had been pretty hungover, so we didn't spend long, just cruised home along Insurgentes, under the chilly gleam of the malls and the top-less bars' warm neons, the brake lights of other cars twisting in ribbons along the windscreen.

Carlos poked at his tuna sashimi. 'I don't know, vato, I can't finish this. Looks too much like chunks of tongue.' He held up the plastic tray. 'You want it?'

'Got my hands full.' I toasted him with a coffee cup that I'd poured my miso soup into.

'That shit is so distracting.' He peered into the cup. 'Look at all those spores. I can hear them bloom.'

A song by Daso was playing low on the speakers, the bass slamming my thoughts to a slow-floating powder. Up ahead, the windows of the Edificio Canada looked like punched-out teeth. Router extension cables poked out around the shards. A cardboard cutout of Wonder Woman bolstered one smashed pane. Other gaps were draped with towels, bedsheets, drying clothes.

Carlos had gotten his second wind, was munching his way through the rest of the sashimi, looking at his Twitter.

'Holy shit, that Baumgartner guy. Remember him?'

'The guy who jumped from space, or whatever, wasn't it?' I said, breaking eye-contact with Wonder Woman. 'A four-and-a-half-minute drop. I watched the whole thing. I was in the pub.'

'Four minutes. No mames. And I mean, if it takes you more than, like, a second? To finish falling?' He pulled a face. 'Man.'

'You'd be in an absolute tatter.'

'How long were the 9/11 guys falling?' Carlos pocketed his phone and put his hand on the back of my headrest.

'I don't know. Fucking ages.' Stopped at the lights, I reached out with my napkin, dabbed a grain of rice from Carlos' moustache. 'Bugging me since San Ángel, that was.'

'God, I would hate that.' Carlos wiped his face with the back of his hand. 'Knowing you're going to die, not being able to do shit about it.'

'Absolute shite craic.' I balled up the napkin, dropped it into the footwell.

We dodged off Monterrey, into the quiet back streets of La Roma.

'What'd you do on 9/11?' I flipped the indicator.

'Let us go home early. Didn't say why. Didn't tell my mother, played some football, went home, found her distraught. You?'

'Home early, same as you. Meatballs for dinner. Felt bad about eating. Mostly just felt sad they'd cancelled *The Simpsons* to put on the rolling coverage.' I picked a fleck of tofu from my back tooth.

'Unforgivable.'

Through the windows the cobblestones were seamed with yellow light.

'Love it round here.' Carlos eased his seat back. 'Like a cake baked to look like a neighbourhood.'

'Then this bit.' I raised a finger from the wheel to point at the long canyon of towers along Reforma. 'Like *Blade Runner*.' My other hand was on Carlos' collar, his nape warm against my forearm, my fingers moving in his hair. 'Those weed brownies I made came out OK. Tried this savoury pastille thing, manchego and chipotle. Not bad. We can go back to mine for them.'

'Sweet,' said Carlos, his hands behind his head.

At the next traffic-lights, Carlos snapped a picture of a fire-eater, a half-nude man painted metallic silver all over his body who blew a huge 'S'-shaped flame into the drizzle above our stalled car, and the memory broke at the thought of how it had all ended – a motorcycle roaring into the fog, throwing fantails of rain over the windscreen, Carlos' middle finger aimed backwards at me, and then coughed-out lung-blood on the walls and floor of Carlos' apartment, the comet-trail of his brain matter streaking the floor – and I pulled in at a petrol station, stocked up on Marlboro Red and donuts and not one but two acrid Americanos. The first drag zapped me like a cattle-prod.

A couple of late gulls flung past as I drove, dried salt whorling their grey wing feathers. The draught of a sixteen-wheeler shook the car on its axles, sloshing coffee onto the seat.

'Motherfucker,' I said, not sure if I meant the driver for spooking me or myself for filthing up the car.

Next headland I came to, I pulled in and parked and stubbed out my cigarette. Pipistrelles zipped past on the gusts, as light and black as ash; fog caught in wet beads on the windscreen. Across the bay, the lights of Buenos Aires were a mesh grid, the donut filling frozen to a slush in my throat. A gentle shirring sounded low overhead. The drone's lens flashed in front of me, but I blinked and it was gone. The noise stayed, though, looping in my head like it would never stop, and I gawped at the surf, donut after donut going down entirely untasted. Lightning dropped from the dry air, set a plane tree on fire. Still munching, I watched the branches crackle and vanish, watched bark peel off and blacken to nothing. Carlos crouched at the foot of the tree, reaching into the hoop of wood where the tree's bole had been, scooping out a slurry of rotten leaves, the lights of my car shining through the bulletholes in his hands, his chest, his wrists.

Both my coffee cups fell into the footwell, leaking their dregs.

'Motherfucker,' I said, then drove to the meeting with those cups rattling around my feet, the noise of the drone from earlier shirring in my head, too loud for even the noise of my car-engine to swallow.

The road took me past the lake and the carpenter's shacks on the shoreline, with their tin roofs and tattered Uruguay flags. Their windows glowed. Flakes of salt were storming down, blown in off the sea, the sludge darkening my Redwings on the short walk between the place I'd parked and the meeting-room, which lay behind a narrow door, between a vegan taco place and a cereal café, under flat yellow lamplight that lent the room the vibe of an off-the-grid laptop repair

33

shop. Although most of the heat came from all the bodies crammed in on old school-chairs, and the coffee looked like the dredgings of a sick river; although the mugs were all crizzled, and the supply room with its copies of the Big Blue Book and the anniversary key-chains and chips lay behind a ratty curtain that was in fact just a ratty Fireman Sam bedsheet, if you say the word *home* to me, even now, it's pictures of that room and dozens like it that pop up in my head before any house, any apartment, any shape on any map.

When I got in the door, I was about ten minutes into the shares, so people just craned and waved or gave nods and thumbs-ups. Marcela, a chemist from one town over, was catching us up on her last trip to hospital.

'Honestly, whatever they put in my arm,' she was saying, 'it just went through me like *uff*, you know?'

A couple of people chuckled.

'And so, you know, obviously,' she went on, 'that shit in the drip was mild as hell. But it nearly blew the top of my head off. Had to lean forward, head between my knees, counting breaths, saying "*Trouble always passes*".' She clicked her tongue. 'So much of this recovery life is just waiting. And there is this gas-leak of need just constantly hissing its way out inside me, and all it needs is one tiny little spark for everything to go *boom*, sky-high.' She tutted again. 'Some truths, you're just not ready for them,' said Marcela. 'And that's usually when your Higher Power hits you with them.'

A van pulled up outside, headlights sweeping the room, and my back jerked straight. But it was just Sancho, getting a ride from his business partner.

Marcela took off her glasses, brushed away a tear. 'And I accept I did so much damage to my body, when I was using. But it just doesn't seem *fair*. You know, you get clean, you do the work. And then what?' She tossed back her hair. 'It keeps you safe from exactly nothing. You just get more shit. Makes me want to throw the whole fucking thing out the window.'

Raquel handed her a tissue. While Marcela spoke, I looked at the patterns I'd imagine shaped out by the black streaks of wear on the floor – the Last Supper, Androcles pulling the thorn from that lion's foot, Baucis and Philemon turning into trees. It helped me listen. There was always a lot of emotion in the room, and that'd make my fingers start clenching on the air, make my toes grab at the insides of my socks, make me start seeing people's faces morph into screams, into masks of weeping, make me see their limbs float off and whack around the room. The trick was to either look at the floor or count down from forty to zero. Mostly that was enough to wait out the hot threat of tears or screams. Sometimes I'd put my sunglasses on. They were sunburst Aviators, garish as hell, like Gaddafi's, if he'd gotten into vaporwave, but that kind of thing only doesn't look weird in places like an NA room, where nobody mocks anybody for anything.

'But I won't,' Marcela said, stooping to collect the blue '*Just for Today*' mug that stood by her ankle. 'Whatever good I had, it came to me from the programme.' Her fingernail ran along the crack in the mug. 'Living right is hard in ways nobody else sees. But even so, it's good to be sober, honestly. How I'd be, in this situation, still using?' She shook her head.

'Probably I wouldn't even have gotten this far.' Her smile fixed itself to both sides of her mouth, didn't make it to her eyes. 'But, hey – good to be clean, good to be in a meeting. I'll pass.'

Listening to her had the inside of my chest feeling like scrunched-up tinfoil. Tonight was going to be a sunglasses meeting.

'Thanks for being here,' said Guillermo, an Argentine air-force vet of around sixty who ran bike tours around the countryside. He'd rattle off the Twelve Traditions at a drill-sergeant's pace, his military boots planking down firm on the lino at the end, but he had the biggest heart in the room.

'Sorry I'm late,' said Sancho. 'Cow issues. Does anybody else want to share?'

'My name's Andrew,' I said, 'and I'm an addict.'

'Hi, Andrew,' said the room.

'Just thinking about the past, is all.' I dropped my eyes to the floor, shuffled in my seat, made eye-contact with Andro-cles' lion. 'Feels like it isn't over, sometimes, or like it's all about to happen again, like the past feels more real than the present. Ten years, five years, six years ago, whatever, they feel more recent than, say, this morning.' I scratched under my chin, seeing Carlos and me in his El Paso hotel room, grey fog coiling under the arches of the international bridge. 'And, you know, that adrenaline life, it's so addictive, part of me wants it again, you know?'

'*The story of my life*,' Carlos was saying, barbed wire caught in the reflection of his glasses, '*and I'm missing it.*'

Sancho tutted in sympathy.

'There's a friend here,' I said. 'Visiting. And she really reminds me of all those times. And I hate those times, and I miss them, too. It's really fucked, she's had something terrible happen to her, and part of me, like, envies her? I don't know. Really bad.'

The damage in the floor turned smoky, morphed slowly into a scene from a Children's Bible version of the Book of Daniel – Shadrach, Meshach, and Abednego battling to stay upright in the furnace.

'And that's even though things are good now, honestly,' I said, my eyes shifting to a tile that looked like King Midas weeping and glowering at a bunch of grapes that he couldn't eat. 'Like, quietly good. But good. And that's obviously my cue to want to tear it all apart. Typical addict vibe.'

The pictures in the floor blurred.

'It's OK,' said Raquel, but she was talking to Camilo, the emotional support Pomeranian she was training.

My beard rasped under my hand, and I was gearing up to keep sharing when the plastic shutters rattled backwards and boots squeaked on the wet lino.

'Sorry I'm late,' said a northern Mexico accent, and I looked up to see a face that stopped my share dead and turned my spine to water.

7

That square beard with no moustache, those punch-blunted knuckles, those eyes as cold and dark as river-pebbles – they belonged to a man who'd kidnapped me not once, but twice. The last time I'd seen him, he'd pointed a gun at me and pulled a sack marked CAFÉ DE CÓRDOBA over my head. There were nights that the smothering taste of hemp and dust and dried coffee woke me, flailing under the covers.

The eyes of the room were on me, nodding me to go on, but I couldn't – not with him there.

The newcomer turned his gaze on me, gave me a backward nod and a shit-eating grin, then screeched out the chair right beside mine, shook raindrops from his hat and squeezed them from his beard.

Sancho said, 'Andrew?'

'Sorry.' I coughed, delved in my pocket for a Kleenex with one hand, batted the air with the other, didn't have to feign the strangle of fear in my voice. 'Mind if I just leave it here?'

'Thank you, Andrew,' said the room.

'Thank you, Andrew,' said the man sitting beside me.

'Would the newcomer like to introduce himself?' said Raquel.

He doffed his cap, and ran a hand over his scalp, and I took off my sunglasses. Between his fingers I counted the tattoos: a spiderweb, a large blackletter 'Z' inked around a map of eastern Mexico.

This was the closest to an oasis my life ever came, and now here he was, pissing my history into it.

He didn't say, '*My name's El Prieto, and I'm a fucking murderer.*'

He didn't say, '*I burned people in their beds, I had men shove body parts into fracking wells, I drowned workers in oil-wells, and I more or less put a gun in this man's hand and got him to help kill for us.*'

What he said was, 'Hey, so, um, my name's Marco.'

'Hi, Marco,' said the whole room but me.

He swallowed, sighed through his nose in a way that sounded genuine. 'And, you know, I'm an addict, an alcoholic, whatever other labels you guys have got going on.' He pointed at himself with both his index fingers. '*Boom*, that's me.'

My knuckles whitened around the edges of my chair.

'And so, I'm just passing through here, know'm saying?' said Prieto, accepting a styrofoam cup of coffee from Marcela. 'Long flight. Lot of time to think. Lot of time to drink. And it just really hit me. Way I'm doing things, I just have these really fucking deep-seated – what'd you call 'ems, character defects? And so we come in to land, and I'm just thinking, before I even go do what I got to do here, I need to get me to a meeting, know'm saying?'

'Thanks for coming,' said Raquel.

'Yeah,' I said. '*Marco*.' My voice was tarry with fury.

'Traditionally,' Raquel said, 'the newcomer is the most important person in the room. Maybe you'd like to tell us what brought you here?'

'Oh, I'd love that,' Marco said, scratching the back of his head. 'Truly. But I guess I'm a bit scared of being in a group, you know?'

Raquel laughed. 'That's why we're all here, really.'

He smiled at her. 'Sure. And don't get me wrong, you all seem really cool, know'm saying? But if I could just run a couple things by an older hand, then maybe come in?'

'I'll jump,' I said.

My tone snapped everyone's head round to look at me. Even Camilo the dog stopped his fidgeting.

'It's no problem.' I blunted the edge in my voice, got to my feet.

Marco scrambled upright, pulling on his cap.

Guillermo watched us through his glasses as we left the room, but, when Prieto turned his smile on him, he dropped his gaze to the ground.

'Nice vibe in there,' said Marco, switching to English, as I pulled the shutters closed behind us. His hand landed on my shoulder and squeezed.

'Where is she?' I hissed, and threw his hand off me. 'What did you do to her?'

'Whoa, man.' He raised his hands. 'Cool it. Do to who?'

'Maya,' I said. 'You followed her, didn't you?'

He frowned. 'What?'

'I saw you. At the airport. You're following us.'

'No, cabrón, we're following you. She's a bonus, I guess.'

'But the needle. The harassment. When she was in Veracruz.'

He just looked at me.

'That is ringing exactly zero fucking bells for me right now.'

'Then who did it?' My hands caught him full in the chest. He didn't budge.

'That had absolutely fucken nothing to do with us. If it was anyone, it was the governor's people.' He knocked me off my feet with a slap to the chest. The wind went out of me. 'And I advise you not to throw hands at me, neither.' He blew smoke at me. 'Motherfucker.'

'I can't believe you'd do this,' I said, on my knees, getting my breath back. 'Your name's not even Marco.'

'You don't know that, man.' He sounded hurt. 'That "Prieto" shit, that's a nickname the papers made up.'

'How'd you find me?' I said. The rain blasted me in the face.

'What's it been? Six months?' He shook his head. 'And not even a "hello".'

'How?'

'Ways and means, cabrón.' His lighter sparked as he lit a cigarette. 'We've even tracked your *jogs*.'

In my head I saw the gear room in the Torre 1521 – banks of monitors, screens showing feeds from military drones, cables like a nest of snakes.

'Hey, where you going?'

'Food.' I was walking towards a sandwich cart whose lights glowed yellow from one street over. 'If I don't eat, I smoke.'

A TV above the sandwich cart's hot-plate showed a repeat of the PSG game. What I'd have given then to be at home, with you and Maya, the three of us carping at the screen.

'Egg sandwich, please,' I said to the woman tending the hotplate.

'No meat?' Marco said. 'That's not a sandwich, man.'

'I can't eat dead things any more,' I said. 'Thanks to you people.'

The first time he'd kidnapped me, he'd dragged me to a redbrick house in the wastes of Veracruz, where his friend had shoved me face-first into the mess that remained of the man who'd murdered Carlos. The metal taste of his blood and brains attacked my palate even if I walked down the meat aisle of a supermarket.

The woman held up a pinch of tomato slices and lettuce.

'Yeah, slap it in,' I said. 'And what sauces have you? Anything spicy?'

The woman's face became regretful.

'Ah, don't worry about it.'

Marco eyed the menu, scratching under his chin.

'How the fuck do these people use the word "sandwich" for these miserable-ass combos. I don't know how you live here, cabrón.'

'It's been a hard six months,' I said, as the woman handed me the sandwich.

'Yeah?' Marco had the note in her hand before I could get my wallet out.

'No, you asshole.' I added as many pickles as would fit under the bread.

Marco was turning a Delicado between his fingers, facing the rain so's he didn't get smoke on my food. He offered me the pack.

'Fuck you,' I said, but took one, and we walked back to the seawall.

Marco looked at me through the smoke that leaked from his mouth, said, 'So, you ready to talk or what?'

'You said you'd forget about me.' I wiped spray from my forehead, leant my knuckles on the brick top of the seawall.

'Mentira, güey.' Marco huffed out smoke. 'We told *you* to forget about *us*.'

'I thought it was over.'

'It's never over, cabrón. We did you a favour, letting you go.'

'And I did you a favour, writing that story.'

'Yeah, and that just invites another fucken favour, man, know'm saying?' He clicked his fingers. 'It's a, what do you call 'em, virtuous circle.'

'I'm pretty sure that's not what that is.'

'Sure it is, man. We got what we needed, you stayed breathing et cetera, win fucken win.' Marco cocked his baseball cap back and leant on the railing beside me, the cigarette puffing between his lips. 'See, you weren't quite the complete fucken liability my boss expected last time out, yeah?' He blew smoke out the side of his mouth. 'Helped our Hail Mary pass out, big time.'

The water was a fat-tongued slopping beyond the railings. All I could think of was the leftists that the cops used to kidnap, drug, tip out of their helicopters and into the water.

'Plus, you know, you're a ghost now,' he said. 'No home address, no bank account, no name on any bills.'

Waves lapped. Shingle rattled. A foghorn blew.

43

'Physically, you know, you ain't going to win any heavy-weight bouts, but you don't really need that shit when you're a good shot.'

For a second, I wanted to dive out of Marco's grip, swim until I was too knackered to stay up.

'Plus, you know, that moral compass you've got, the one you pick up in journalism?' He huffed out a laugh. 'The one where you tell yourself you're "one of the good ones"? Like a cop does? That shit, it makes you perfect for the job, far as I'm concerned.'

If I drowned myself, you'd be in the clear, and maybe Maya, too. But you knew how drowned people looked, so, if I drowned myself, I'd hover in your head forever, nude and bluish and fish-nibbled, my jaw slack, my eyes bulging with the salt shock of water tearing my lungs.

My head dropped forward. Rain blitzed the back of my neck. You always think you're ready for these things until you're about to do them, and I saw the mess of blood on Carlos' apartment floor, heard the forensic cleaner who'd scraped him into a binbag saying, 'No self-defence injuries, one attempt to escape – I've never seen a victim so calm.'

Yeah, well, he'd been calm because he'd kept me safe from everything he knew. But there was no way I could keep you safe.

Prieto's hand slapped my neck.

'Ain't like you have a fucken choice here, cabrón, know'm saying?'

His fingers tightened.

The surf boomed. The bridge of my nose felt like it was going to fall off, I was pinching it so hard.

'Yeah, yeah.' I waved a hand. 'Alright.'

'That's my boy,' said Prieto. He patted my back. 'Hey, just think of that lovely intact house of yours. Think how you'd like to keep it that way. Makes it easier.'

The lights were milky on the churn of rain and waves.

'What do I have to do?' I said.

'No biggie.' He offered me another cigarette. 'Mostly, it's just you keeping this friend of yours safe.'

The cigarette dropped from my fingers, bounced into the sea.

'No. No way.'

Marco held his hands up, smiling a little.

'Whoa man,' he said. 'This is very much a vegetarian-type assignment, know'm saying? Kind of thing she'll be real into.'

'There is no way I'm dragging her into this as well.'

Marco turned those river-pebble eyes of his on me.

'There very much is a way.' He reached inside the pocket of his hooded jacket and took out a tablet, then swiped the screen.

The footage was pristine, HD, 1080p, showing you pacing around the kitchen and sitting room, your hands on your head.

'Oh,' Marco said, wiping a drop of rain from the screen. 'Not looking too happy. Wonder why.' He pinched the screen, zoomed in on the kitchen table, and slowly the three dark rectangles lying there resolved into the acid blotter, the printout of Julián Gallardo's face, the copy of *Proceso* with Carlos on the cover, even the white seams that had formed in the cover from all the folding and unfolding.

A feeling like iced water bucketed down through me.

'You broke into my car?'

'Gotta get you better at covering your tracks, cabrón.'

'Where's Maya?'

'Oh, I ain't got a camera on her.' Prieto swiped shut the tablet and slid it back into his jacket. 'I ain't some kind of pervert. But what I *do* have, on your *house*, right, is that fucken drone, and that fucken drone has got a couple things on it that if I just – *drop* it,' his hand jabbed the air – 'right onto your roof?' He mimed an explosion with his spread fingers.

There was no point in struggling in his grip, because there are fridges that weigh less than Marco did, but I struggled anyway.

'Man, really?' He just sighed, squeezed harder, and shoved two fingers from his other hand into my throat, right behind my collarbone. The pain took my knees from under me, and I leaned over the rails, trying not to be sick. The woman at the sandwich cart was craning over to see what the noise was. Marco raised a hand.

'Something went down the wrong way,' he called over to her in Spanish. 'No offence to your sandwich.'

A long string of spit that tasted of bile broke from my lips and into the waves.

'What do I do?' I said. My voice was a beaten croak.

He gave a chin-jut in the direction of the ferry-port.

'Hotel over there,' he said. 'Go brief your friend. Give her this.' He held an envelope out between his fingers. 'You remember my boss?'

In my head, I saw Puccini and me sitting on a fallen pillar at the El Tajín pyramid, the glare of his jeep's headlights falling over us, as he told me his story – how he'd gone to the US to provide for his family, how his daughter had been an A-student, how she'd been kidnapped and made the slave of a young gangster neighbour, how he'd taken her and her baby daughter to Guatemala because the police couldn't keep her safe, how he'd started working for the governor of Veracruz to make sure she had too much money and security for anyone to ever go after her again.

'Vaguely.' My mouth still tasted horrible, and I spat again. The rain and fear-sweat had me soaked altogether.

'No need for sarcasm, cabrón. You remember his daughter?'

'Yeah – and his granddaughter, too.'

'Yeah, her.' He pointed at the envelope. 'She must have heard about all this shit with the governor running to Guatemala, because she upped and vanished like a week ago.'

'Why'd she be afraid of the governor?'

'Because he is a stone psychopath, man.'

'And that's coming from you.' I got to my feet.

'What's that supposed to mean?'

'Nothing. I still don't get it.'

Marco squinted at me and tapped a cigarette against the box. 'How good a lawyer you think the governor has?'

'Good enough to get a plea bargain, I guess.'

'Precisely, cabrón.' His eyes moved over the waves and he shook his head. 'That motherfucker, he's going to sell every one of us down the river if it'll stop him going to jail. Me, Puccini, the whole team. And, you know, me? I'd shoot

47

myself in the head, I thought there was no way out. All's I got's my wife and all. No kids.'

'But Puccini's not like that.'

'No. A family man. The governor gets his daughter, he will flip right away. And she cannot guarantee her own safety way he can, so that's where we're needing you.'

'Christ.' My hands were working through my hair, a tangle snapped against my fingers.

'You find her,' said Marco, and offered me another cigarette, 'and you bring her to him. Y ya.' He clapped his hands together. 'You are out, free to go now in peace to love and serve the Lord.'

'And you can't do that?'

He scoffed. 'Us? Wandering around Guatemala City in broad daylight, knocking on women's shelters and everything like that?'

'Alright, alright.' I lit the cigarette with the lighter he gave me. 'So we're camouflage.'

'Now you're getting it.'

'And so my friend does what?'

Marco shrugged. 'She just does her thing. Finds the girl, talks to her, gets the story out, story about how the governor's a threat to her life, all this shit, so that there's enough noise around her that the governor can't do shit without there being a big fucken smoking gun leading all's the way back to him.' He shrugged. 'That's the lógica, anyways.'

'Sounds a bit – uh, I don't know. Improvised.'

'A bit uncharacteristic of the bossman, you're saying?' Marco leaned his hands against the railings and sighed. 'You're

48

not wrong, cabrón. But, you know, family gets into a thing, shit gets like that.' He shook his head, then reached into his pocket before handing me what looked like a clear plaster, still in its wrapping. It was about the size of an earlobe. 'Anyway, back to it. You stick this to your friend's bag, or her shoe, or whatever, and we're able to see where she goes, decide whether we need to keep her safe, stuff like this.'

'That doesn't sound too safe to me.'

Marco shrugged.

'Given the shit she's been digging round in, this is 'bout as safe as it gets. Closer she is to his daughter, closer she is to being safe. Plus, you know, only way the governor stays in jail's if he can't sell anyone to the DEA. Because there's not a cell south of Nuevo Loredo'll be strong enough to hold him.'

The bug rested on my fingertip. It was see-through and wobbly, like a contact lens.

'Don't put it on a wallet,' he said, 'or on a phone. Some shit with the magnetic strips and stuff, it'll fuck it up.'

A wind could have blown the bug away, so I zipped it into the back of my wallet.

'Couple last things.' He swung a small backpack off his shoulder and unzipped it, then handed me a plastic case about the size of an iPad.

For a second I just looked at it.

'C'mon, cabrón, open it, don't stand on ceremony, it ain't fucken Christmas.'

The box clicked open, and I jerked my head away like the inside of it stank.

'Oh, Jesus.'

'Don't be a pussy.' Marco tutted. 'Ain't like you ain't fired one before.'

The Glock handgun gleamed out at me from the egg-box lining of black foam, so clean and black and shiny that it looked like a hole in matter, just a straight-up gap on nothing.

'Lot of ordnance for a vegetarian-type assignment,' I said.

'Yeah, well, her assignment's not all you'll be doing.'

'And I get to know what the rest of it is?'

'Nothing you ain't done before.' Marco's fingernail tapped the barrel. 'Plastic. Won't show up on a scanner or any of that shit.'

'Nice change of subject,' I said. 'And the bullets?'

'Once they're in the gun, you're good. That shit it's made of, it's got something in it fucks with X-rays or whatever, makes them show up as something else, I don't fucken know. And we got to workshop your shooting a little. You got to stop doing the fancy shit.'

'"Fancy shit"?'

'Yeah, cabrón, like that shit where you shoot out the fucken tyre of a car, know'm saying?' He tutted. 'Fucken chance in a million shot and you go for that. Bullshit. It ain't got to be hard. You shoot the biggest part every time, whether it's a car or it's a person or whatever.'

'The windscreen, then.'

'Yeah, now you get it. And with people, it's between neck and feet, squeeze two, three times, bam, bam, bam, and then make yourself small and fucken *run*.'

The half-busted sodium lights ticked. The gun shone under the light. My stomach flipped slowly over.

Marco took out a second, slightly larger case. 'And this thing. Fuck, am I glad to be dropping this on you.'

The case nearly yanked my arm from my socket, it was that heavy.

Prieto pointed.

'And do not open that here, cabrón.'

'What, is it a bomb?'

'What? No! It's for the bullets, man. You wear it. There's two of 'em, one for you, one for your friend. They're just a fucking bitch to fold flat. That got you less worried 'bout your friend or what?'

'Not massively, no.'

'Ah, there's no pleasing people, I swear to God.' He rubbed his arms. 'Fuck, man, how long you gonna keep me out here? Shit's cold. I'm a desert man. Can't deal with this rain shit. Worse than fucken Veracruz.' He held up his car keys. 'Ride?'

'Jesus.' I flinched. Last time I'd seen him with keys in his hand, he'd chucked them right at my temple. 'Yes, as if I want you to see where I live.'

'As if I don't fucken know already.'

'I'll drive myself.' I wiped my fingers on a napkin. Those pickles had been dribbly. 'Need to think up a cover story for the partner, don't I?'

'*Tss*,' he said. 'I know that feel. Just stay as close to the truth as you can, man.'

'And then?'

He raised his hands. 'Just stand there and take it, man.' He adjusted his baseball cap, gave me a nod, and patted me on the shoulder. 'You'll do the right thing.' He pulled up his hoodie. 'I'll be back.'

On my phone, there was a string of missed calls from you, and a voice-note from Maya.

'Just a heads-up,' she said. 'Things got a bit intense at home, yeah? And so I've, like, checked out of your place. Sorry. It's just with this news about the governor flipping me out, and your partner flipping out, and my editor flipping out, I don't know, I'm going to cool it for a couple of days, get a bit of space. Hotel I'm at's the one right by the ferry-port. It looks a bit sex-hotel-y, and I, like, don't hate it? Which is to say, you would probably love it. Anyway, uh, yeah, if you're still alive after you get back home to whatever's waiting for you, and you need to talk, or whatever, I'll drop a pin so you know where I am. Good luck, yeah?'

There was no point putting it off, so I pocketed the phone, turned my back on the sea, and started walking.

Passing the food-stall on my way back to the car – the game was over, apart from the bickering of the pundits – I threw the napkins overhand into the bin, muttered, 'Three points', and stepped back into the rain, my collar up. The chucked-away bottle-caps were a tiny galaxy under the streetlights. Cars slushed past. Rain traced vein-shapes over the cobbles. For a while it was almost cinematic, but then the panic shut on my chest again, and I was just wet, and cold, and alone.

8

When I got home, you were sitting at the kitchen table.

'So, you cracked, too,' I said.

You didn't say anything, didn't even look up – just sat there, your right fist clasped in your left hand. There it was, everything I kept hidden in that car – the *Proceso* with Carlos on the cover, the photo of Julián Gallardo and his peeled-off face, and the blotter of acid tabs lying between your elbows.

'All of this was sitting on your side of the bed. My mind went to all the obvious places,' you said. 'That the news triggered you, made you relapse, whatever, I don't know.' You shook your head. 'And you come back, making a joke out of it?' You pushed the blotter across the table. 'How often are you taking the tabs?'

'I've stopped.' I flopped towards the table, got to a chair just in time. 'I swear. Since the day I met you, I haven't taken a single one.'

You shook your head. The lamplight caught a shine of tears on your eyelashes.

'So what are the tabs still doing around here, then?'

To be fair, you were right to get upset about the acid. That stuff had me fried long ago. Even now, when I think of my brain, it's like that infomercial from the '90s – you know the one, the one with the egg hissing and spitting in a pan of oil, except what I see is a kilo-odd of pink mince being scooped out of my head and into a searing hot pan, where it sizzles, browns, smokes. When I think that way, I have to lay my hand on the top of my head, to make sure the bone's still sealed.

'I don't know.' I lifted the blotter, ran my thumb over the joins between the tabs.

My eyes tracked over the room. Your photo of a Portuguese Man-o'-War legion caught the light. You'd told me about seeing them off Venezuela, about how they'd leave whole schools of fish stewed to a goop of softened parts, about how sometimes big octopuses would rip off their poison tentacles, flail them at sharks, and the rest of the creature would just keep right on drifting, unfazed.

'You miss it, don't you?'

My eyes flicked to yours.

'Miss what?'

My voice was too stony to sound like mine. That happened a lot. Mostly I couldn't tell whose voice that reminded me of. But tonight I recognised that hard note from the way Marco talked to me.

'Don't use that tone on me,' you said. 'I won't talk to you if you use that tone on me. We've talked about this.' I shifted the blotter, the *Proceso* with Carlos on the cover, the photo of

Julián Gallardo until all three faces looked like a cutaway of one head.

You pushed the magazine at me. Carlos stared up at me from the cover. 'And you miss him, too. Don't you?'

My foot tapped the floor and I started to count the taps down from forty until the wish to cry went back in, except my head kept stopping at thirty-four, and that sting in my eyes, it wasn't going anywhere.

'This the bit where you tell me I need to see someone again, is it?' It wasn't my voice at all any more. It was the voice I'd hear when Carlos got drunk and ratty and tried to blow everything up. In my head, I pictured those Man-o'-Wars and their whips of ripped-off tentacles.

'Fuck you. I don't need to listen to this,' you said.

Yeah, that was something I used to say when I was fighting with Carlos, too, during those awful battles where we'd pull everything apart, blow it up, make a crater of our relationship, find ourselves too exhausted afterwards to do anything apart from put the word 'reconciliation' on our own tiredness.

You pulled a bag from under the table.

For a second, I envied you. That was a trick I'd never pulled on Carlos. Maybe I should have. Maybe he wouldn't have wound up dead. And OK, so I'd never have met you, but it's not like I got to keep you, either, so what's the point in going down that road?

There was a flash of pain and I heard someone scream, heard glass crash, heard wood snap, heard you yell. Next thing I knew, you were standing by the door, saying, 'It isn't safe here for this kind of conversation. I want you gone.'

'Do we get to talk about this?' I was clutching my wrist. The pain had my voice sounding all wispy. My knuckles stung. Your face looked fine. That was good. That meant I probably hadn't hit you, just hit the picture beside your head.

'We just did,' you said.

'Love you, too,' I told your back as the door shut.

9

You leave home as often as I do, you never really unpack, because you never know when you might have to do it again.

And I've done it so many times now, I could do an advice column about it.

First, you tweezer the glass out of the back of your hand. If you're angry enough, you won't feel a thing. You take your iPad and your laptop and your little plastic briefcase with the pistol in it and your little metal one with the bulletproof vest in it.

You pack your most weatherproof jeans, your most boring T-shirts, your last partner's jumper and your dead partner's leather jacket – against outdoor cold, in theory, but most likely just against sleeping-in-your-car cold.

After that, you take your dead boyfriend's ashes from the envelope, nick a Ziploc from the pantry, and tip him down the funnel for recycling cooking oil. When he's safely gathered in the bag, you slit open the lining of the jacket and gaffer-tape the bag into place, so that it's hanging by the hard rim of sealing plastic at the top of the Ziploc, and then you sew shut the tear so that, with the jacket on, he will fit snugly right over your heart.

Sit, then, for a while, smoking under the Edison bulbs, staring at photos of Man-o'-Wars, at the high-definition waves, at the acid pool the colony leaves behind – bone-pucks, husks of scales, tissue reduced to syrup – and at the star-shaped crack marring the glass of the frame, feeling the sting of the cuts in the back of your hand, watching your own blood darken the bandages.

Wait until a spike of pain stabs through your head, then press the heels of your hands against your eyelids, until those Man-o'-War colours bloom up – electric blue, livid purple, deep, blood-spill red – and become all that you can see.

10

The door buzzed.

'Unbelievable,' I said, as I opened the door.

'Sorry for your trouble, man,' said Marco, his baseball cap over his crotch, his head bowed. 'Saw the whole thing on Drone-O-Vision. Mic's pretty good, too. And the heat-mapping. Body language told us a lot.'

'"Us"?'

'Oh, just me and the drone.' He stepped inside. 'It's not like I'd spread your shit around.' He blew on his bare hands. 'Wouldn't say no to a coffee, neither. Shit is *cold*, cabrón.'

Wordlessly I went to put the kettle on, then leaned against the countertop, my arms folded.

'Nice place you got here,' he said. 'Whole thing's a real shame.'

'It is.' I reached into the cupboard, towards the French press.

'So,' Marco said, 'you got a type, or?'

The question made me reach past the French press for some treacly, awful instant coffee instead.

'So's I can hook you up,' said Marco. 'See, I'm open-minded.'

'Like –' I sucked in a breath, counted back from forty, got to thirty-nine before the twitch in my eyelid made it impossible to continue. 'You know what, it's easier to just say "*thank you*".'

Marco's mouth hung open a little.

'Sugar?' I said.

He jerked his head back, saw the spoon in my hand, said, 'Oh. Yeah. Two. Please.'

'What was it you had for me?' I poured boiling water onto the granules. The crema looked like an oil stain, that's how 'emergency' this instant was.

Marco unzipped his backpack, slid out a stiff manila folder. 'Ferry tickets.' He lifted them onto the back of the open flap. 'One for you, one for your friend. Ferry leaves in four hours.'

'Bit rushed, no?'

'Well, I'd say so.' Marco nudged my seabag with his foot. ''Cept for you've already packed, ain't you?' With his knuckles, he tapped a laminated sheet with a QR code printed at its centre, the address of a private hangar underneath. 'Don't lose this. Pain in the ass to get it to begin with. Show it to the dude by the fence. There's a charter hangar – he'll be there, he'll scan that square thing, you'll drive on through and park.' He shut the folder and replaced it in his bag, then took a large gulp of coffee. 'Y ya. I'll see you both on the plane.' He gave me a salute. 'Good luck convincing your friend. Hope she goes easier on you than that partner of yours.'

'Thanks.'

'No sweat off my sack, cabrón.' Marco drained his cup, put on his baseball cap, and headed for the door.

'Well, you'll be keeping an eye out, so I'm sure I'll be fine.'

Marco looked not a little wounded.

'Harsh, dude, real harsh,' he said, and shut the door behind him.

When he was gone, I went to get the car keys, then stopped, thought for a second, and went to Maya's room instead. She'd left the elephant candle behind, and I pulled the mattress needle from its flank and slipped it into the bottom of the gun-case. Then I took the house keys from around Carlos' old Fidel Castro keyring and left them on your table, and walked out of that house for good.

II

My route to Maya's took me past your hotel, and I parked on the square with its statue of Artigas. The dog from the beach was asleep under the bench, beside the brown Labrador who'd been mauling your firewood that first morning, while I sat there huffing your smell of gardenias from the scarf I was still wearing, wishing I didn't have to breathe out, wishing my own frightened sweat wasn't already replacing those traces of you. The light was off in the room you and I had slept in that first night. After a last look at the dogs and that dark window, I kept going.

The place where Maya was staying was right at the dock. The Buenos Aires ferry glowed on the black water. Cranes swung in the pre-dawn gloom. The receptionist must have been told to keep an eye out for me, because she waved at my approach and laid a key-card on the desk.

'Room 504,' she said.

'Thanks.' I took the card with my weaker hand. My knuckles were still leaking through the bandages. I texted Maya so she'd know it was me coming to the door and got into the lift.

The corridor to her room was like walking inside a vein, just this tunnel of red light, with a throb of techno playing softly on speakers that I couldn't see. When I swiped open her door, she was sitting on one of the twin beds, tugging at a hangnail with her teeth and peering at her laptop screen. A busted light kept flickering outside the window, its buzz as loud as a mosquito.

'Everything OK?'

'See for yourself.'

She turned the screen around. I looked. The floating cobalt gaze of my old cat, Motita, looked back. She was lying on her back in a soft white basket. After Puccini's people had trashed my apartment, I'd had to leave her with Maya, even though they'd never gotten on. Thankfully, though, the security guard from her building was more of a cat person: there he was on the screen, feeding her chunks of croissant, his smile wide enough to show his braces.

'Living the life I couldn't give her,' I said, stretching out on the other twin bed, my bleeding hand hidden in my jacket pocket.

'Worst father ever,' Maya said.

'Oh, so suddenly she's growing on you?'

'Yes,' she said. 'Look at that beautiful resting bitch-face.' She shut the laptop. 'I take it things didn't go so well for you after you got back.'

'Ah.' I took my hand out of my pocket without even thinking. Probably I wanted to scratch the back of my head or something.

63

'Neta?' Maya said, when she saw. She shook her head. 'Qué chingados, güey.'

'It was a wall,' I said. 'And then a picture. Relax.'

She swatted the air at me. 'That's still fucked up, yeah? Jesus.'

'First time it ever happened. Even with Carlos.'

'That should worry you.'

'Oh, it does.' The hand twanged. 'Ah, Christ. I think I broke something.'

She reached over and took my wrist, studying the wrap.

'You get all the glass out at least?'

'Ah yeah. I wouldn't like to be careless. I like that hand. I use it all the time.' I sat forward on the bed, my elbows on my knees, and huffed out a deep breath. 'But here, I need to level with you – there's way more worrying stuff going on.'

'Is it that phone call? The one earlier?'

'Kind of.' I stood up. 'Have you one of those little coffee-station things?'

'Andrew.'

'Alright, alright.' I sat back down. 'Look, remember that night when Zúñiga got himself killed?'

'Yeah.'

'And you remember how, like, I warned you to get out of your gaff, and go over to my editor's house? To Dominic's? So you could hide, or whatever?'

She nodded.

'Well, how do you think I knew?'

Her hand slowly lowered from her mouth. 'You were – Jesus. I can't even say it.' She was on her feet now, all the way across the room, her hands raised, her face twisted with disgust.

'I was involved, yes.'

'Don't even fucking speak, yeah?' She leaned against the windowsill. 'No chingues.'

The buzz of the light made my scalp itch. I clasped my head and leaned forward. My jaw clenched so hard that I felt my skull hum.

The TV was on, showing a news item about Amazon's warehouses, the corridors between shelves shot from above, wedged tight with brown packing envelopes. Now and then a gift-bag flashed purple in that river of brown. That image made me dizzy enough to grab my seabag like I was about to wash away.

'Hey – are you listening?' said Maya. Her voice reached me all blurry with echo, like I was underwater. Then she seemed to notice something about my face, and the anger went out of her look, and turned to something a lot like fear.

'I don't know.' My face was burning. So were my eyes. 'I wish I knew what was wrong with me but I don't. I never have. I don't know. I'll never know.' Something in me wanted to club my knees with my fists, like that might beat the pain out.

'Hey.' Maya crossed the room and sat down beside me. 'I get it. It sucks. It was a hard time. You were confused. But – come on. Helping fucking *narcos*?'

'That's not the worst of it.'

Maya was looking at me sidelong.

'They sent you, didn't they,' she said.

All I could do was nod.

'So you're threatening me,' she said.

'No! No,' I said. 'Jesus. Low blow.'

The backs of her knuckles struck my shoulder. 'Here I am, bouncing from one threat to another for as long as I remember, yeah? And I come here, trying to get *away* from all that shit, and then it turns out that the one person – as in, the actual literal *one person* that I think I can trust – is out there working for these bastards *all along*?'

'It wasn't all along. It was just once. And it's not like I had a choice, either.'

She threw up her hands.

'Yeah, like, my poor heartstrings. Like they'd kill a foreign correspondent.'

'*Former* foreign correspondent.' My fingers stroked back and forth against my temples, hard. My skull felt like it was about to pop open.

'Well, what, then?'

'They were my sources. They kidnapped me. They admitted to everything. And then they got me an interview with Zúñiga. Without them, there'd be no article. And without the article, Carlos –' My hand flapped at the air. 'Oh, you know.'

'Carlos would have died for nothing.' Maya's voice had gone quiet. She was looking at the cases on the bed – the one with the gun and the one with the bulletproof vest.

'You know how this works,' I said. 'All those people, the ones you met, the ones running the Oxxos and the taxi-ranks, all the money-laundering fronts – you know they don't want to be there. You know they don't have a choice.'

'Plata o plomo,' she said, touching the case with the gun in it.

Silver or lead, a bribe or a bullet. You take one or you get the other.

'And now I'm in it, too,' she said.

Once again, all I could do was nod. I took out the ferry tickets. 'We're to get the ferry to Argentina, then take a flight to Guatemala City. After that, you find Puccini's daughter, and then you interview her, and then you publish it in your paper.'

Her eyes narrowed at me. 'And that's it?'

'That's it.'

She frowned at the gun-case.

'That's a precaution,' I said.

'That's kind of them. But it's funny, you know, all this.'

'Sort of.'

'No, no – not like that. Just as in, a funny coincidence. Because my editor, on the phone? He was, like, excited, yeah? About all this shit with the governor.'

'To be fair, Daniel can be a bit fucking galaxy-brain about stuff, at the best of times.' I knew her editor a bit, a silver-fox type, all slacks and skinny ties, like a tidier Jarvis Cocker, except hepped to the gills on Earl Grey the whole time, and absolutely not louche at all, with his cheesy Fonz finger-guns and big-picture angles that were never worth the trouble.

She bobbed her head side to side. Her eyes were still on the case.

'Well, yes and no. Like, OK, he's miles out of touch, or whatever, but now and then? I don't know. He hits on something. And I mean, you know, I just want to go to sleep for a week. But he was, like, seeing some opportunity in it, or whatever.'

'What'd he say?'

'That with the governor on the lam, it "expanded the scope of the book", or whatever. Because we needed "restitution for all the victims".' She was putting on his voice, doing air-quotes with her fingers. 'And that meant, like, looking into Guatemala, specifically. On account of that's where he re-cruited a lot of the Zetas from, right? And the daughter of one of his employees? If she talks, that's, like, a super-rich angle, yeah? Because she's a victim of all this, too.'

'So you don't have a problem with where the tip is coming from any more.'

Maya made a face. 'Touché, or whatever, but it isn't as if the whole thing isn't entirely morally questionable, either, yeah? I mean, I went to Chilpancingo a while ago, and the kids there were charging five hundred pesos to tell their stories.'

'You're the staff writer,' I said. 'Just expense it.'

'Well, that's the thing,' she said. 'I nearly had to, in the end. Because none of the kids would talk for free, because there's this, like, union of kids, yeah? Who beat the shit out of you if you talk for free. So I just wrote about kid sicarios charging five hundred pesos to tell their stories, didn't I?'

'Fair.'

'Besides, you know, this is a good thing to do, in terms of helping people, yeah? Because she'll want to talk, to keep her father safe, and her kid safe, and whatever noise it makes puts more pressure on the authorities to get the governor.

68

And that's what everyone wants. And so this?' She tapped the case, shrugging a little. 'Well, it's kind of a two birds with one stone type of thing. We get ourselves out of trouble. And we help my book along.'

'You're starting to sound worryingly like me.'

She picked up the ferry tickets.

'There a way to change my seat on this? Away from you?'

'Open seating.'

'Alright, now I'm in.' She folded her ticket into her pocket and got to her feet. 'I'll pack my bag.' She slid her laptop into the zip-up case. 'You didn't tell me what they want *you* to do.'

'Oh, who knows,' I said. 'And I don't really want to ask.'

'Do I want to know why they picked you for this job?'

Carlos' body on its stretcher, rattling down the stairs of his apartment building, blood-darkened strands of his hair overhanging the blanket. 'Because they know I won't let myself lose another one,' I wanted to say.

But 'Not really, no' was what I said.

'And after that? After I find the daughter? What do you do then?'

'No idea,' I said. I got up from the bed, and went looking for a kettle and some coffee.

Maya went into the bathroom and started running the shower. The coffee made, I stood over her handbag with the bug Marco had given me on the end of my fingertip. He'd said not to stick it to her phone or her wallet. A voice-recorder would probably mess it up in the same way as a phone would, I figured, picking it up and dropping it again. Her comb slid out of place, so I put it back in and felt something slide and bump my hand – the little donut-shaped wallet where she kept her Citalopram.

'Perfect,' I said, and stuck the bug to the inside lining.

'Did you say something?' Maya said from inside the shower.

'Talking about the coffee.' I zipped up the donut and dropped it into her bag.

'I hope you were being sarcastic.'

I was sitting on the bed, the case with the pistol open on my lap. The gun was light in my hand. Underneath it, folded into the cutout, was a belly-band holster. After loading the magazine, I tied the corset-strings snug against my navel, the holster pressing on my tailbone: hours earlier, I'd put these jeans on to go to a Narcotics Anonymous meeting, now there was a gun in the back of them, because *normal* can mean just about anything you want.

12

Maya and I drove onto the ferry, then made our way up to the faux-granite bartop and even fauxer chrome of the coffee-dock. The bluish glow of the fly-killer lights shone down on us. Maya turned to the menu's drinks pages.

'Which of your cocktails is the most efficient?' she said to the woman behind the bar.

'Say no more,' said the woman, and whisked off to the bottles.

'I *like* her,' Maya said to me as I sat down on the stool next to hers. 'Why are you wearing sunglasses? It's six in the morning.'

'Eyes are sensitive.'

'But it's dark out.'

'They're sensitive to questions.'

The woman returned with a highball.

Maya put the straw in her mouth, then stopped. 'Wait – you don't mind, do you?'

'Nah.' I took out my keys, showed her my six-month chip.

'I thought you had more time than that.'

'Yeah, like, I think the whole "taking acid for days" thing required something of a restart.' I put the keys back in my pocket. The Fidel Castro keyring clinked against them.

'Ah. And so?' She raised the glass again.

'Do it for me.'

She took a sip. 'Oh wow,' she said to the woman behind the bar. 'What's in this?'

'I can never remember,' she replied.

We took our drinks over to a couch by the window. We hadn't much trouble finding a good spot: the rest of the people on board looked like commuters sick of the view – they were mostly just stealing naps and tapping their phones. Maya's drink had her out for the count before she was even halfway down the glass, leaving me to take in the look of your town as it drifted away from me. The bay shimmered under the morning light, and the sky went on forever. It was like a reshoot of the morning you and I had gone out in a yacht lent to you for the day by a guest. We'd ridden the drag of tugboats and dredgers all the way around Buenos Aires, getting greeted with honks by the ferry crews, fresh gusts pummelling me in the head as we veered past the blue domes of the Russian Orthodox Church near San Telmo, before cruising on to Montevideo, to your father's bookshop, just ahead of another evening of that unsettling sleet we'd been getting, watching it come down with him in the sea-cave dimness of that old pink townhouse. Its outer walls had been so worn they looked like a lumpy cake, the inner walls lined with books, a real *Swiss Family Robinson* feeling to it all, even down to the pallet of rescued books in the corner – some of

72

them succumbing to damp, all of their spines seamed with white creases, the cloth bindings frayed, the pages sallowed by time and the drag of hands, the tight crawls of script like maps of a very dense city – then joining your mother in the warm yellow glow of the kitchen, where all four of us had looked out the windows, down at the yellow solder of street-lights melting into the gaps between the cobblestones. My body rocked in the remembered motion of the water under our boat all that endless, perfect day. It wasn't long before I needed the sunglasses again.

'Hey, I asked you what's *wrong* with you,' said a voice behind me.

When I looked up, I saw that the voice belonged to a sharp-faced girl of about seven leaning over the divider between her banquette and mine.

'Well,' I said, easing back in my seat, but then the girl's mother hooked her from view with a cross word.

'I just keep thinking,' Maya said, 'about that migrant story. The one we did.'

'Yeah.'

'Two years we spent at it, on and off, wasn't that it?'

'Up and down the country I don't even know how many times.'

The pictures were still bright in my mind – glaring sun over the migrant shelter at Ixtepec, the slap of suds at the concrete sinks of the laundry room, the overloaded clothes-lines; the chains of people walking the verges of the highways, their trainers slowly falling apart, some of them hobbling on crutches, their burst heels like peeled tomatoes.

73

'The place I keep remembering is that train-stop outside Apizaco,' Maya said.

'Jesus,' I said. 'Yeah.'

Apizaco was a sex-trafficking hub – still is, actually, it's been one since the time of Cortés – and Maya and I had gone down there to talk to people staying at a shelter that was just behind the train-tracks, videoing testimonies from Central American women about how they'd been captured on the road, put to work in table-dance bars, in brothels, in private houses, trying to pay their fare north. As we'd been leaving, part of the La Bestia train was slowing to a halt, its hiss of brakes like a dragon exhaling. There weren't many people on board – the company had made the ladders smaller that year, bought in containers that had curved roofs, so there were fewer places for migrants to climb onto – but there was this one family all packed into the covered gallery at the back, four kids, a mother, a father, and two large men dressed head to toe in black standing over them with AR-15s cradled in their arms, the light winking on their wraparound black sunglasses. They saw Maya and me and gave us a long, slow nod, the pair of them.

'Those two guys,' Maya said. 'With the guns. On the train. And now we're going on a plane with someone just like them.'

'Honestly,' I said, 'you tell yourself "This isn't really happening" enough times, it starts to feel true.'

Behind the bar, I heard someone clank coffee-grounds from the espresso machine into the bin, and it all came back to me in a rush – the hipster coffee-shop in Mexico City, the barista called Leo who'd been a driller in Poza Rica, and who'd had to feed the body parts of indigenous people and activists and whistle-blowers into fracking wells while Marco and another Zeta called Mangueras had held him up at gunpoint.

'Doesn't any of it matter to you?' Maya said.

'Afterwards I was too wiped out to move,' Leo was telling me in my head. 'All I could do was lie there, cooling my belly on the bathroom tiles.'

'Sometimes,' I said.

'My being alive was just an accident,' Leo was telling me. 'The thought was exhausting.'

I wanted to tell her about him. I wanted to tell her that you can't recover from a thing like the one he'd been through – or like the things I'd been through – because you can't even try, you just shunt yourself onwards, lessened, punctured, quietly a wreck. On the outside, it looks a lot like peace. Really, though, it's just devastation.

But I said nothing.

Maya was looking out the window, nibbling at the tip of her thumb. After a while her blinks got longer, until finally she slumped down along the seat, her cheek resting on my shoulder. With my eyes shut, the warm rise and fall of her body against my arm could almost have been you.

13

Off the boat, we took the bus-lanes all the way to the private hangar. Container lorries rumbled past on either side. The car's tyres hummed in the silence. No security kiosk stood by the gate to the hangar, only a guy with a scanner in his hand, his sunglasses and his cagoule hiding most of his face. He said nothing when the scanner beeped green, just hauled open the gate. Up ahead, Marco waited, his hood up, his hands in his pockets, his feet in their fat Nikes stamping the concrete. A swoop of dread went through my body when I saw him.

When Maya saw him, I heard her breath go in, hard, heard her seatbelt pull taut.

Oh, she knew him, alright, knew him from police mug-shots and news reports, from rumours of student massacres and the photos Carlos had left for us on his USB stick.

Maya turned towards me, her mouth open a little, and I could feel the weight of fear and loathing sliding down through her body, because it was sliding through mine, too.

Marco walked across the concrete. He took off his cap and opened her door. Maya stayed where she was, her handbag held up like a shield, her face a mask of disgust.

'Real sorry to be discommoding you like this,' he said, reaching a hand to help her out. He'd put on a gentle voice that made him sound like an overeager waiter at a bad restaurant. 'But we'll keep you safe. You're gonna be a great help to us, know'm sayin?'

'That's a shame.' Maya got out of the car, walking past him to a plane that stood behind Marco. It wasn't much bigger than my Impreza.

'In *that*?' I said.

Marco looked over his shoulder and nodded sullenly.

'We get a stopover in Cartagena. Great vending machine in Cartagena.'

Another guy in a cagoule drove a buggy-sized tow-truck across the runway.

'Does everything have to be hobbit-sized?' I took the cigarette that Marco offered me.

'It's the budget, cabrón.' Marco bobbed the Delicado between his lips. 'We're having some personnel issues. Otherwise, you wouldn't even *be* here.'

The second cagoule guy got out of the buggy, connected a hook to the front of my Impreza.

Marco flicked his eyes away from me.

'You people are in trouble, aren't you?' Carlos' old Fidel Castro keyring spun in circles around my index finger.

Marco breathed smoke out through his nose. He looked as tense as I was feeling.

'Shit is not ideal, cabrón, let's just say that much.' He jerked his head at the stairs. Maya was already walking up them. 'C'mon now, let's get this over with.'

I followed him up the stairs and stooped through the door, into a space of grey pleather, thick with a male fug of beer-sweat, piss, the shoe-leather hum of machaca. Maya was sitting in the back row of the three, her arms folded, staring out the window. She didn't look at me when I came in.

Marco settled into a nest of games cartridges, charger cables, and inflight blankets that were scattered across both his seat and the one beside him. 'You get hungry, there's stuff in the fridge.'

'No way.' I said, lifting a Krispy Kreme box from the stack in the crisper. Styrofoam boxes of ready-meals were stowed in the main part. A microwave rested on top of the fridge.

'Be sure and you empty that shit all out before we land. Ain't like you're paying for it.'

The pilot climbed the stairs parked in front of the cockpit. Marco leaned back in his seat and turned to Maya.

'So, this gonna be your first time in Guatemala or what?'

She ignored him.

He sighed and turned back around.

'Alright, be that way.'

The engines began to whirr. Slowly we taxied down the runway.

Marco slid a joint as short and thin as a dart from his inside pocket.

The whirr became an overdriven roar, and then came the jerk of take-off. A trapdoor seemed to open in my stomach.

For a moment I prayed the wall of the plane would cave in, right where I sat, sucking me into nowhere, but then the plane banked, levelled out, and I let go of the dream.

Marco lifted the joint in a wordless question.

'Honestly, man, you could do lines off my back and I would not feel tempted.'

His eyes narrowed.

'What I'm saying is that you can smoke it, it doesn't bother me.'

'Sweet.' He lit up, took a long drag, then offered it to Maya. She looked back and forth between him and the fuming end of it for a moment, then said, 'Fine', and took a drag.

'Well, thank God,' Marco said. 'We can all be friends.'

'Don't push it.' Maya handed him back the joint.

Marco slid a pair of white headphones over his ears, picked up his PS4. 'You need anything, I'll be here.'

I got a coffee from the machine by the fridge and ate my donut. Through the window, the clouds were grooved with pressure, shot with light. Powdered sugar caught on the sweat above my lip as I chewed and swallowed, made me think of the sweat on Carlos' lip, one of the evenings I'd rescued him after his benders. He'd called me from a payphone in Parque Delta and told me to meet him at the food-court, right by a Chinese restaurant so cleared out by the weekend crowd that only the saddest fried curls remained in the buffet tins.

'Nice boa.' I slid into the chair beside his.

'Thanks,' said Carlos. 'Shot it myself.' He sighed and shook his head. 'Shit, man, I'm so sorry.' His face looked as sickly as a Caravaggio under the fly-killer lights.

'Do I want to know how you wound up here?'

He sucked air through his teeth. 'Patchy footage, vato. After-party in Cantinita 22. After-after-party in the dark-room – pretty sedate. After-after-*after* party at this bar on the Alameda – El Internet, the place is called. Met a guy. Sorry.'

'Whatever.' These slips of his, I'd learned to look past them. His reasonings were always long and never worth hearing, as though the point was to weary me into forgiving him.

'Well, OK, so we got back to his, and he wanted to show me these videos. Thought it'd be porn. It was him chainsaw-ing a man into six pieces.'

'Jesus.'

'Yeah. Ran out of there so fast I left my wallet behind.'

'Your wallet's on the table.'

'OK, so I just ran out of money. Ah, so . . . ?' He pointed at a tray littered with napkins and coffee-soaked pastry crumbs.

'Right.' I took a two-hundred-peso bill from my money-clip and slipped it under the saucer of his coffee. 'You need a shower or anything?'

Carlos nodded. 'Change of clothes'd be good, too.'

'Sure.' I lifted the Soriana bag I'd brought, with some of the bits and pieces he'd left at mine.

Carlos looked into the bag, let his mouth fall open.

'You are a lifesaver.'

'Yeah, well.' I twirled my new keyring – a white one, from N.A., marking my first six months – my first first six months, before my relapse with the acid. 'Ride?'

'Oh, man.' He drained his coffee. The big-eyed look on his face hovered somewhere between baby wolf and needy kid. 'That would be extremely badass of you.' He wiped his mouth with the back of his hand and got up so fast that his chair nearly fell over. 'Shall we?'

Through the plane window a puff of cloud dimmed the sun for a second. My face loomed up in the glass, looking as bad as Carlos' had that day, bags under my eyes thick enough to sponge up floodwaters, and so I pulled down the blind.

Marco yawned, woke. 'Man,' he said, his arms folded, his eyes puffy, 'really is one of those days when all's you want's a blowjob and a torta, and you'd settle for the torta.'

'You're going to have to.'

Marco pulled a horrified face and got up. He pissed with the door open. I heard Maya shift in her sleep.

'Bit of a lightweight, your friend, huh?' he said.

'She's been stressed,' I said.

'Ain't the only one stressed round that town, I'm thinking. Kicked you out pretty fast, partner of yours, am I right?' he said over the rumble of his stream.

In my head, the jet engines thoomed, burst, slowly cooked Marco to the fuselage.

'Yeah, well, all that small stuff you don't notice, it builds up.' I imagined the sizzle of his body-fat, the glopid sputter as he burned.

'I hear that,' said Marco, stooping to zip up his fly, as though his dick was just that heavy. 'Still, that shit looked salvageable to me, cabrón.' He shook first one shoulder, then the other until his in-flight blanket dropped over him just right. 'Me and my girl, we've had our shit to work on. Marriage, man.

81

It's work. It's just that you both have to want to do it.' He settled his head on the pillow, then frowned a little, and grabbed
two more pillows from the seat in front of him. 'Use this,' he
said, 'as an opportunity for growth, know'm sayin?' He shut
his eyes. 'See you in Cartagena.'

Not long after he drifted off, Maya unclipped her belt and
slid into the seat beside me.

'What the fuck,' she hissed. 'What the actual fuck.'

'If it's any consolation,' I said, 'he's mellowed since last
time.'

'I don't want to hear about your disgusting, macho fucking
murderer friends.'

'You're hungover.' I flicked a hand at the fridge. 'Get
something to eat. I know how you get.'

'This is the worst thing anyone has ever done to me.' But
she got up, went to the fridge, and slid a styrofoam tray into
the microwave. 'Oh, and I suppose you'll want one too,
won't you?' She clattered in a second tray, or at least tried
to – styrofoam doesn't really clatter.

'Mine has a "V" on it, I think.'

'Such a fucking diva.' She switched them around and
slammed the door. Marco kicked in his sleep. Both she and I
looked over, startled, but he didn't move any further.

'Just think of it as another interview,' I said, as she sat down
beside me.

'No. Not one bit of this is alright, and you know it.' She
wagged her fork at me. 'You can argue this any way you want.
But you're sitting on this plane, and you're sitting on the
fucking *mounds* of bodies going back to the eighties that these

people have been heaping up, yeah?' Her fork hit the table and skittered onto the carpet, landing right beside Marco's foot. 'I don't know how I can even *eat* this.'

'Here.' I picked up her fork and wiped it off.

'What are they paying you?' She took it.

'I'm alive, aren't I?'

Maya looked down at her food.

'Fuck,' she said.

'It is what it is.' I pulled down the blind again, then stretched as much as those shitty seats would allow.

'I'll let you sleep.' Maya lifted her tray.

'Alright.' I zipped up Carlos' jacket and leaned against the wall beside my seat. 'We OK, then?'

'Less not-OK,' she said, and slipped out of the row, back to her seat. 'Maybe.'

14

Somehow I managed to sleep through the stopover at Cartagena, so I never got to see the famous vending machine that Marco had mentioned. When I woke up, I could see through the clouds. The rim of volcanoes could have been Mexico City, and so could the air-pollution tints staining the sumac and fir and oak in the parks below us, to the point where I got a leap in my chest thinking I was back home. But then I heard Marco stir and grunt in his sleep, I remembered everything, and the sound that my throat made was too angry to be a sigh, too tired to be a groan. My hand had seeped during the trip – the bandage was almost black – so I got up to change the wrappings in the bathroom. Little flecks of glass were still caught in there, and I tweezered them out with my Leatherman. Through the door, over the rumble of the engine, I could hear Marco's halting attempts at conversation and Maya's curt replies.

'Nice to see a bit of bonding going on,' I said, coming out of the bathroom, as Marco handed me a cup.

'Oh, fuck you,' Maya said.

Marco snickered.

'She didn't know shit about your secret employment,' he said.

'I wasn't sure how comforting it'd be,' I said.

'The stuff about being a good shot was, a little,' Maya said.

Marco clicked his tongue.

'Hey, I said lucky, not good.'

The seatbelt light tinged on. Marco shifted in his seat, reaching for his belt, and said, 'Christ, this shithole again.'

The plane lowered through the banks of cloud. The city was a flat-roofed nowhere of concrete and smog stretching out on all sides. We bumped onto the runway, then rolled to a halt. As we stopped, a Garifuna kid drove a stairway up to the door of the plane, climbed it, popped the door open with a hiss, then pelted off at a run before he could see our faces.

'How's the vending machine here?' I said to Marco.

He clicked his tongue. 'Sorry, cabrón. There ain't one. Now, c'mon.' He whacked my back. 'Let's get rolling.'

Climbing down the stairs, the pollution taste of each breath felt like a papercut. The outlines of the volcanoes shimmered silver in the distance.

A jeep with tinted windows waited for us at the foot of the plane, so new it didn't even have plates – just a printout taped to the back window. Nobody received us. The keys were in the door. Inside, the cold buffets of aircon hit me as a relief. Marco's banda playlist did not.

'You couldn't dial down the "desert man" stereotype, could you?' Maya said.

85

Marco tutted but took the blare down a couple of notches anyway.

Traffic was thick, but his driving was quick, agile, a lane-to-lane shimmy, one second riding the tail of a red pesero, the next hanging off the bumper of a MetroBus, and then veering back in front of cars to honks and cries of 'Chinga a tu madre!' from the other drivers. Driving around, it was hard to tell the old buildings from the ones that just looked old from all the smog – the stone townhouses tattooed with soot, the keeled-over balcony-pegs, the gate-posts rusted to the texture of coral, planks as dark as sea-wood barring empty doorways. On the walls, the plaques showing the streets' former names were scrawled out by dead ivy.

The road dived through a section of tunnel painted with shoals of mackerel, before rising onto the new highway to Antigua, looking down on a horizon dog-toothed with ware-houses and cement plants and smokestacks. A mile and a half out that other road took us into a whole other city – rooftop gardens, furniture shops selling diamanté mirrors and Roman busts and leopard-print everything, past tall electronic ad hoardings that showed white celebrities running their hands along sofas, banisters, cream-heaped frappé cups, down a forested track towards tall stacks of yuppie hutches that rose out of fir and balsam trees. Marco slowed towards a modern white house in a lot of its own. Even through the windows, I could hear the hum of the electric wire running around the perimeter wall.

'Welcome to your house,' Marco said, pressing a button that made the gates whirr backwards.

'Thought the budget was miniature,' I said.

'Oh, it is.' He drove us through and parked beside a yellow Crossfox. 'We own this from before.'

The gate clicked shut behind us. We got out of the car and Marco carried Maya's bag for her to the door. The scrubby hills glittered with uplit swimming pools, white-walled villas, houses like glass and metal clouds resting on stilts.

The earth smelled dry as chalk. Even out here, the pollution smarted in my nose. Every breath gave me the squirmy chest-pain that I remembered from Mexico City, days when the air makes you think 'What's the point?' about quitting smoking.

Inside the house was a space so minimal and empty that it felt like stepping into a beige fog. L-shaped white couches sat in front of a flatscreen, and the kitchen had a fridge like the big obelisk in *2001: A Space Odyssey*. The high shine of the floors made them look laminated. On the wall hung pictures of dramatic Guatemalan landscapes that had been built over by now, or else were ragged-looking with single-use plastics, or else smothered under the smokes of some US-owned maquiladora. Everything inside was pristine, but the bad air outside had yellowed the windows.

'Right, I'm out.' Marco left a gate key on the kitchen island, right beside a block of about a dozen knives. 'You see me again, it's because you've fucked up.' He was looking at Maya.

'And when am I getting out of here?' Maya looked at him with her jaw set.

He stepped towards her. A cold feeling rippled along the back of my neck. For the first time in hours, I was afraid of him. My hand found the stock of my pistol. My heart knocked in my throat.

'You don't find my boss's daughter, you don't get out of here.'

The colour went from Maya's face, but she didn't back down.

Now Marco rounded on me, his nostrils flaring, his eyes gone from river-pebble cold to the smoulder of coal.

'Keep an eye on her, cabrón,' he said. 'Or it's both of you going in the hole.'

He shouldered me out of his way and breezed past me out the door, slamming it behind him. Maya and I stared after him until the car engine turned over and the electric gate rattled open.

15

'Fuck.' Maya sat down on the shorter leg of the 'L', her head in her hands. I crossed the room, found a goblet in the cupboard, filled it with water.

'Here.'

She glugged down the water so hard that some of it spilled on the floor.

'Oh, what do we do?' She slapped her hands to her forehead.

'We do what they tell us, then we hope for the best.'

Keeping someone else calm can only keep you so calm, though, and my bones suddenly weighed a ton with the exhaustion of having to deal with all of it. I fell down onto the couch beside Maya.

'I hate this,' she was saying. 'They could get us to do anything.'

'Just focus on what they're actually asking.' I opened my satchel and took out the envelope Marco had told me to give her. 'Look – here's the start of a lead.'

She opened it.

'This is just the name of an NGO,' she said. 'And her name.' The envelope flapped to the tiles.

'You don't need much else.' I robbed her water, drank the rest of it, but the dryness wouldn't go from my throat. 'It's more than you start out with most of the time.'

Maya looked at me.

'What?'

'Do you ever wonder if you're – maybe, just a little – minimising the scale of this thing?' she said.

'Often. But look.' I scooted in closer and slid out my laptop. 'Did a bit of homework for you on the plane. So you'll be out of here faster.'

'You found the daughter's Facebook?' Maya put her glasses on. 'She has one? That's pretty stupid.'

The top of the page read Estefany Martínez. Her photo made her look like she'd had an emo phase in her teens, one that had left a deep mark – the lip-ring, the black streaks dyed through her red hair, the oversize glasses. She looked happy in the photo, and so did her kid, whose long arms and legs and big smile made her take after her mother a lot. Knowing what I knew about her life, it gave me a poignant sort of a stab under the ribs to look at them, and to think of all the madness they had to put up with.

'She wasn't hard to find,' I said. 'She has Puccini's real name down as the father in her "FAMILY" section.'

'Are you fucking kidding me?'

'I don't know. People do stupid things when they miss someone.'

Maya craned to look at the screen.

'Doesn't say where she's living, though. She's not *that* stupid. Sadly.'

'No need to worry there. Look.'

Scrolling down, I found a photo of Estefany from about a year before, smiling bashfully up into a camera that caught more of the restaurant's lamp-flare than it did of her face. She was holding hands with a clean-cut-looking guy in a blue floral shirt, tattoos peeked out of the cuffs and spilling over the backs of his hands. Estefany's small daughter was doing peace-signs at the edge of the picture.

'They're kind of cute,' I said. 'Don't you think?'

Maya sniffed.

'They look like they met at some kind of born-again evangelical shithouse for kids done bad.'

'You're being mean.' I cropped a screenshot of the boyfriend's face and did a reverse image search.

The boyfriend's Instagram popped up. So did the address of a tattoo studio. I wrote it down on the back of a Krispy Kreme napkin that I'd taken from the plane. 'You want to make those calls to that NGO, and that convent, and see how far you get? And we'll go see this boyfriend or whatever, in case you wind up going down a dead end.' I got up from the couch, stretching again. 'Think I want a shower. I smell like plane.'

Maya looked up at me. She was scraping her bottom teeth against her thumbnail. The fridge motor clicked and restarted in the silence.

'Don't take too long,' she said. 'It's fucking creepy down here.'

★

After showering, I lay on the bed a while with the TV on, showing 'explosive fire events' wracking Alta Verapaz – shots of blackened forest, drought-parched fields, date palms turned to ash – while I looked at the gun in my hands, tried to get used to its cold weight, tried to figure out the things that all the switches did, but all I managed to do was tip the bullets right onto my belly and wind myself. When I'd gotten my breath back, I practiced my draw by springing out from behind the door with my finger on the trigger, one eye shut, the sight of the muzzle shaking on a point above the bedside lamp. At my ninth try, the door to my room opened, and I slammed myself against the wall behind the door.

Maya poked her head into the gap and said, 'Uh, what the fuck are you doing?'

'Ah.' I rocked on my bare heels, my gun-hand behind my back, leaning my elbow against the wall to keep from falling over. 'Yoga?'

She frowned at the arm folded behind my back.

'Yes,' I said. 'I'm not very good at it, like.'

'I see,' she said, doubtfully. 'Well, uh, I got on OKish with this UN migrant shelter, or whatever. They're not, like, utterly against letting me in.'

'So that's promising.'

She weighed it up with a movement of her head.

'I mean, yeah, but I'm not going to sit around waiting for four days with that fucker breathing down my neck, when they might just say no. And that's assuming they even let me talk to her. What if they just fob me off on some randomer?'

'That'll be enough.' My back was starting to shake. 'Long as you interview someone in the place where the daughter's at.'

Maya's eyes narrowed.

'Why? They bug me or some shit?'

'I don't know, I'm just going by what they told me.' The lie slid down my gullet, a greasy weight.

'Yeah. Well. I don't know. Part of me wants to go talk to this boyfriend, or whatever. As, like, backup.' She gave a backward nod at me. 'So, you know, you want to put on something more formal than a towel, maybe?'

'It does seem like a special occasion.'

'Right, well, I'll see you downstairs.'

'Sure.'

Her head withdrew from the gap, the door clicked shut, and I slid down the wall to the ground, let the unloaded gun drop into my lap.

16

The kid's tattoo studio was at a 'commercial and cultural space' in what passed for the capital's hipster district, just off the plaza near the Congreso, where an older man wearing a faded Real Madrid baseball cap collected twenty quetzales from me for moving a couple of bricks out of the only parking space left. We walked along the railings where monochrome photos from some Ministry of Culture exhibition about the Civil War had been hung.

'Hey, I'd heard of these,' Maya said, pointing at the images. 'They're stills from a documentary, about this guy working in the Interior Ministry tipping off people who were on hit-lists before the government could get them.'

'Feels weird to hang those pictures there,' I said. 'What with Congreso voting to make the war happen.'

The pictures showed stuff I'd only seen in history books and old news articles – assault rifles nudging young women in the kidneys; students in bloodied shirts leaning their hands on the walls, their heads stooped in post-torture exhaustion.

'It was really hard to get those images,' Maya said. 'Ministry used to destroy them all.'

A kid held up her bandaged hands to show the camera the place where her fingers had been. Families pressed torn-off bed-sheet handkerchiefs to their mouths.

'Huh,' I said.

Sectioned limbs lay heaped on wooden walkways, flecked with ash-coloured muck; rot-softened parts were stretchered from a mass grave.

'The narrator of the documentary, she talks about how the reels were all faded, damaged, how she had to rinse off the dirt, clean the pictures back to life, or whatever.'

'Bit like the bodies themselves,' I said.

'She says that, too,' Maya said. 'Very poetic, the narrator.'

The rain-darkened wooden crosses were marked with no names, just HOMBRE, MUJER, a year. The next picture showed a student-age man, about Carlos' build and height, his mouth and eyes pleading, flinging out a hand towards the camera as he was pulled by the waist into the back of an old-style Ford Condor by people the camera couldn't see.

'You look a bit green,' Maya said. 'You want to keep walking?'

'Ah. Maybe a little bit.'

We kept going the handful of blocks towards the tattoo studio, past a book fair watched over by Kaibiles wearing maroon berets and jungle camouflage, P90s cradled in their arms, then through the glass doors and into the cultural space, where the low echoey thud of house music braided around the muttering of a fountain. Tourists and students sat at the long maple workbenches, in the clamshell glow of their laptops.

The tattoo studio was between a red-awning speakeasy and a chai bar. A group of schoolkids was clustering around outside.

'There's no way it's going to happen,' said a man's voice from inside. 'You're not eighteen.'

'C'mon, I'll pay double,' said the tallest of the kids.

'I don't need the money,' came the reply.

'Everybody needs the money,' said the tall kid, his voice starting out strong, then faltering as he realised he couldn't keep his own bravado going.

'Excuse me?' said the man's voice.

The tall kid looked at his feet, shrugging.

'Yeah, thought so. See you in a couple of years.'

The cluster of school uniforms broke off, the tall kid walking with his head down, scuffing his shoes against the floor. Some of his friends looked embarrassed for him. The rest were slagging him off. Maya and I moved towards the doorway of the studio, where the guy from Estefany's Facebook photos was sitting at a desk, copying designs from the big screen of an iMac. The unit he worked in had dark blue walls, and framed flashes hung all around, thick-lined black-and-grey religious motifs, the kind Carlos used to go in for – the stations of the cross in miniature baroque medallions, the scourge and the pillar, the pincers and the crown of thorns. Carlos had that last one around one shoulder. That was enough to make flashes of his other tattoos flicker through my head, the ones on his hands first – praying hands on the left, an anchor wrapping the words NEC SPE NEC METU on the right – and then smoking holes bloomed through the memory of those hands, the letters scorching away to thin tapers of smoke, and the shock of it all shut my throat.

'Hi there,' the tattoo artist said to us. 'You want to make an appointment?'

'Ah, actually, I just wanted to talk.' Maya held up her 'PRENSA' lanyard like it was a cop's badge. 'Have you got a minute?'

The guy laid down his stylus on the design tablet.

'To talk about what?' He pointed at me. 'You press, too?'

'No, um' – I cleared my throat – 'I'll wait outside.'

The guy's brow furrowed. Maya was looking at me with her mouth slightly open.

'OK, man,' he said, with a little shake of the head.

'Sorry about that,' I heard Maya say. She was pulling out a chair across the desk from the tattoo guy. 'We're a bit jetlagged.'

'I can see that.'

I went out of the tattoo parlour and then out of the building, I leaned the back of my head against the wall, lit a cigarette, breathing in drag after drag without feeling a thing. Across the road, on a shadeless square, a scatter of men in their mid-thirties was knocking a scrappy football around near some concrete urinals, topless, skinny-torsoed, their jumper-goalposts mealy and tattered. The biggest one stopped the game when he saw me, gave me a backward nod, raised the heel of his hand towards me as if to ask me what my problem was.

But I said nothing, did nothing, just held his gaze in the reflection of my Aviators, thought of the gun holstered at the small of my back, the stock already skin-warm.

The other four men with the curly-haired guy watched him to see what he'd do. Smoke chugged from my mouth in rhythm with my laugh. The guy with the curly hair still did nothing, so I moved my hand to touch the gun's snug weight. The light was huge around me and I felt towering.

The guy clicked his tongue, dropped the ball from where he'd clamped it under his arm, scuffed it ahead to restart the game, shaking his head, and I went back inside to the parlour. Maya and the tattoo artist were shaking hands at the door of the studio. They both looked relieved. He gave me a curt wave, nodded to Maya, and ducked back into the studio.

She gave me a big thumbs-up as she approached, lowering her voice to say, 'She's been lying. The daughter. She didn't go back to the NGO – she's hiding with the nuns.' She lifted her palm to show me a second address written on the Krispy Kreme napkin. 'Her boyfriend – they're still going out – says the nuns run a tight ship, but they're not assholes about it. He's going to call ahead.' She headbutted my chest. 'C'mon, be excited, yeah? We're almost safe.'

Tyres shrieked against loose grit, right next to us, and I shoved Maya back inside and slammed myself against the wall, the gun suddenly in my hand, waiting for the crackle of gunfire.

But none came.

Our Crossfox slowed around the corner.

'Oh, fuck,' Maya said behind me, clapping dust from her shirt. The security guards inside were craning their heads, and a couple of the tourists had looked up from their laptops.

The window of the Crossfox lowered. Marco was at the wheel. He was wearing a worried look and a black plate-carrier vest.

'We fuck up?' I said.

'No. We did.' Marco opened the jeep's back door. 'Get in.'

17

Maya slid into the back seat, and I got into the front passenger seat. There was a sawn-off sitting in the footwell. 'Oh.'

The accelerator jolted me hard against the seat and we took off.

Every lane of the highway was a grumpy, honking cram of buses, trucks, scooters, cars.

In the rear-view, the two security guards stepped away from the spot where we'd been standing like it was about to blow up.

Marco took a police light from his glove compartment, reached out the window, slapped it onto the roof, and there was a crack that made him jerk his arm back in.

'Puta.' He shook his arm like he'd been burned.

'Are they *shooting*?' Maya turned in her seat.

'Fuck you think they're doing?' Marco jammed his foot all the way down, crumpled the bumper from the Nissan next to us, shoved the car into the oncoming traffic. 'And you do not want to fucken look, by the way.'

Shots chewed up the side door and our window. A car tyre burst somewhere. Marco didn't react, just pushed the accelerator further down until the whole car was shaking like a washing-machine on its last spin. My feet pressed flat against the footwell and my hands against the roof and the rim of my window, like that was going to keep me upright if we flipped.

'Oh, Jesus,' Maya said, lowering her head. 'Where are those Kaibiles from outside the book fair?'

'The guys shooting *are* the Kaibiles from outside the book fair,' Marco said.

Two police cars slid into our lane from the exit above, first one car, then the other, their lights off, their sirens muted.

In the queue outside the MetroBus, a couple of people jerked up from looking at their phones, checking their reactions against other people's. You always get this moment when someone's shooting – that frozen second where people aren't sure what's happening, or else are sure, but don't want to believe it.

A masked cop holding an assault rifle leant from the window of the car nearest us. Gunfire clattered and the people in the bus-queue scarpered, cowering, shoulders hunched, handbags and backpacks and magazines held over their heads, as though the shots were nothing more than rain.

A bullet crumped against the jeep, left a white, star-shaped crack in the reinforced glass, and a heavier thud put a divot in the roof.

Marco laughed at my reaction, gunned the engine, took us through the gap left by the cars that had been revving ahead in a panic. A scooter cut in front of the cop-car, braked, blocked them, and we were gone.

Marco whooped, veered into the MetroBus lane, and glass shattered as a Suzuki Swift jerked to avoid us but crashed through the glass of the platform. People screamed. Some of the glass hung frosted from the ceiling of the platform, but just for a second – the rest of the shards dropped, dashed against the concrete, and everyone screamed again.

Marco cackled. The whine of our engine rose, and I felt the sound along the bone of my forehead.

The police car loomed large behind us. There was a flash and a rattle and the back window spilled over us.

'Jesus!' Maya yelled, pulling her hoodie up as tiny white dice of glass spilled over her. Marco pulled right, mounted the pavement, right through the book fair. People screamed. Tarps flapped. Metal poles snapped. Books and credit-card terminals and loose change flung across the bonnet.

'You going to use that thing or what, cabrón?' Marco whacked the gun with the flat of his hand, then dropped the window for me, and I leaned out, holding the shotgun, the draught and the fear rippling through my chest. The police car was still behind us. Tourists fled. Buskers abandoned their speakers. Two of them fled out of the path of the cop-car and I squeezed off a shot that sparked across the bonnet of the cop-car and almost broke my arm in two, the recoil was so hard. They turned, but too far, and crumpled into the side of a taxi.

Marco clicked his tongue.

'You'll get there.' He patted my leg. 'Don't worry.'

In the back seat, Maya was looking at me, aghast.

Marco cut past a taxi. The driver blared the horn. A draught rocked our car. Marco gave him the finger.

Up ahead a chain of schoolkids was emerging from the book fair, three teachers ushering them across the road, one on the near side, one in the middle, one waiting on the far side. A cop-car pulled out of the cross-street, right behind us. Marco didn't kill the speed.

'Hey,' I said. 'The kids.'

The dashboard hummed under my palms, where I was shoving against it, like that might slow him down.

'Marco!' Maya struck the back of his headrest. 'The kids!'

'I see them, I see them.'

The middle teacher, a woman of around thirty, she looked up, saw us, shoved the girl nearest to her towards the other side of the road.

'Oh, come on, man, seriously,' I said.

But the girl fell sprawling, and the teacher went scrabbling after her, hauling her by her pink Dora the Explorer rucksack.

That left just one boy, standing in the road, his mouth gaping. He must have been about six. He wore a little sky-blue fisherman's hat.

Well, six was about to be all he ever was, I could hear myself thinking, but then the teacher's arm jerked out and the kid was snatched to safety. We sped past, the draught knocking them both flying, and the kid wailed.

'You nearly killed him!' Maya yelled, and hit the back of the headrest again.

'No, I didn't,' Marco said wearily. 'I have parent reflexes.'

The other kids mobbed their friend. The cop-car braked, swerved, crashed into a postbox beside them, and the screams of the kids drowned the clatter of metal.

A toll-pay overpass rose ahead of us, a canal tube below, with roadworks lying abandoned on the loose dirt and sand.

A third cop-car waited for us on the narrow shoulder, another guy in a mask leaning against its bonnet for cover. The muzzle of his gun flared. Silver dimples printed themselves across the bonnet of our car.

'Seatbelts,' said Marco.

The bonnet of our jeep was aimed right at the second cop-car.

The gun swung up and I ducked.

'Seatbelts!' said Marco again.

The cop scrambled for cover.

'C'mon, man.' Marco pulled the belt across my lap, clicked it shut. In the back, Maya did up hers.

The cop's back and head thudded against our bumper. My hands found the roof, the side-wall, and the airbags bloomed open.

Metal crashed. The floor dropped from my stomach and the Crossfox dropped into space.

Two tyres blew out. Our bumper clanged to the ground. Marco whooped again, popped the airbags with the butt of his pistol. The two side hubcaps spun rattling away from us on their rims.

'Ouch.' I cupped my ears.

'Get over it, cabrón,' said Marco. 'She's taking it better than you.'

He wasn't wrong – Maya was leaning against the seat in front of her, braced the way those safety cards say you're supposed to in the event of an air-crash.

In the rear-view mirror, the cop-car teetered in the gap that we'd punched in the siding. At the other end of the canal tube was a long tunnel. Marco rounded a heap of sand and a striped red crash barrier. The blown-out tyres had us careering side to side, knocking over traffic cones, breaking a shovel-handle in two, zipping inches past a dune of gravel chips under a tarp, and I fell back against the seat. Behind us, Maya lifted her head from her arms.

'You OK back there?' Marco said, making eye-contact with her in the rear-view. 'Not hit?'

She looked dazedly from his reflection to my face, then shook her head and settled back against her seat, arms folded.

'Just deaf,' she said.

We shot up out of the gulley joining the canal tube to an upward-climbing road. Ours was the only car, and we were going fast. People tugged back their curtains and eased away from their doors as we passed, because we could be anyone, and nobody driving a car that looked like ours was up to any good. The thing was a wreck, broken glass and shreds of metal rattling in the back seat, stray cables from the charging phones and card-terminals that we'd smashed through trailing across the bonnet and whipping off in the draught, the smoke through the bullet-holes on our bonnet darkening from grey to black. Wind buffeted through the smashed back window, and the shreds of our tyres flapped in loud circles.

The gate of the safehouse clanked shut behind us. The smoke from the bonnet was black now. Marco stopped the car, got out, and ran to the boot for a fire extinguisher before dousing the whole front of the car in white foam.

'Well, go on in,' he said.

We did as he said. The blue dark inside smelled of cigarette smoke. A single light was on in the kitchen, and a man in a police uniform sat under it, half-shrouded in cigarette smoke, beside large platters of cheeses, cold-cuts, halved watermelons, chopped papayas and mangoes, bowls of grapes.

When Maya saw him she turned around, a hand to her mouth.

'Tu chingada madre,' she said.

The man in the kitchen got to his feet. A scar ran down the middle of his face. Under the light, it looked like a crack in a mask. His crew-cut had taken on a lot of grey these last six months, and the relaxed floating bravado of before was gone, too. He ran a hand over the back of his head as he walked towards Maya and me. The look on his face was apologetic.

'I've put you both in a situation of great risk,' Puccini said, in that Southern-US-accented English of his. He'd told me he'd learned it on the building sites in Georgia where he'd worked as a carpenter. It made him sound like a dodgy pastor. 'I can only apologise to you.' He put his hand out to shake Maya's, but she kept her arms folded. He didn't react, just moved over to shake mine, and I took it before I could even think.

'Please,' Puccini said, gesturing to the four stools around the kitchen island. 'Marco, if you wouldn't mind?'

'Sure, jefe.' Marco opened a cupboard and took out a bottle of mezcal. Something that looked a lot like a puff adder was balled up at the bottom of the clear glass bottle. Marco took a glass from an overhead cupboard and poured himself a shot. 'There's juice for you, cabrón. Fridge.'

'As and when, don't hesitate,' Puccini said. 'After the nature of your drive, I'd expect you to be hungry.' He swatted the air. 'Excuse me for smoking so near the food.'

''S'all good.' Marco took up a slice of chorizo and rolled it into his mouth before sitting down.

'There a beer in there?' Maya said behind me, as I opened the fridge door.

'One or two.' Two dozen bottles of Gallo shone up at me, the gold of cartridges. I flipped off the cap of a bottle with the opener on the sideboard, then slammed the fridge so hard that everybody stared. Maya stayed standing as she drank, leaning with one foot against the wall, while I sat at the island with the other two.

'Now,' Puccini said. 'An update, if you wouldn't mind?'

'That NGO you gave us was a dead end,' she said. 'So we looked up your son-in-law. He told us where Estefany is. It's a convent.'

'The one you probably left her at, jefe,' Marco said.

'What's the address, please?'

Maya read it out from the napkin. He nodded.

'Excellent. And have you scheduled a meeting?'

'We didn't have time, jefe,' said Marco.

'I was addressing our colleague.'

Maya gave a backward nod at Marco.

'What he said.'

'These two did OK back there, jefe, eh,' Marco said.

'I assumed they would,' Puccini said. 'But if I'd wanted a comment, I'd have asked for one.'

Marco gave a side-to-side nod like his boss had a point.

Maya drained her bottle and left it on the floor.

'I'll go organise that interview,' she said. 'Means I might get out of here sooner.'

'We can assure you of that,' said Puccini. 'As a matter of priority.'

'I'll believe that if you get me to the airport without getting shot to pieces,' she said from the stairs, and then she was gone.

'Want to make sure she doesn't leave, jefe?' Marco said.

'No, no. She knows better than that.' Puccini cut off a sliver of watermelon, flicking out each seed with the point of his knife. Beyond the platters, I could see three ventilator masks resting on three balaclavas, with a belt of flares next to each one.

'Please, have some,' he said, eating the watermelon off the point of his knife. 'We don't have terribly long.'

'Don't eat too much.' Marco laid his iPad on the table. On the screen was the LinkedIn profile of a light-skinned man in a mid-price suit. The top tab said he was a junior architect at a firm whose logo looked expensive, even if its name meant nothing to me.

'Your dinner date,' Marco said.

'This is disgraceful,' I said.

'You won't be eating together,' Puccini said, giving Marco a warning look, then pointing at the screen. 'This is an architect

for the firm who designed Uruchurtu's property here in Guatemala. And he's expecting a first date with a woman who
does not exist.'

'Big OKCupid fan, this motherfucker.' Marco plucked a
grape.

'We'd like the floor-plan to the governor's ranch,' Puccini
said. 'And we'd like you to encourage him to give this document to us.'

'But gently,' Marco said. 'It's a public place, know'm sayin?
Keep the head cool.'

Puccini shrugged.

'I would say feel free to improvise, since we do need the
document. But perhaps not terribly wildly.' His pauses, his
slow way of talking, it opened up these chilly spaces between
the words.

'Like I said,' Marco continued. 'Very much a vegetarian-
type assignment.'

'And these?' I picked up the balaclava.

'What you think they're for?' said Marco.

'For after,' Puccini said.

'I can guess what they're for,' I said. 'I'm just not really sure
why it's me you need to be doing this.'

Marco laughed. The sound was about as warm as a chain-
saw's slow revs.

'Ain't no*body* else, cabrón. What, you think we got you
in for your fucken O.G. credentials?' Marco said through his
laughter.

'That's enough, Marco,' said Puccini. 'But it's true. There
is nobody left of our old group. The governor has either

bought them, or scared them into hiding, or simply killed them.'

'Three of us,' I said, my hand on my forehead, my hair flopping down, already wet with sweat. 'Against – how many of them?'

'Well,' Marco said, 'it's more like two and a quarter, let's be real here.'

'Thirteen defectors from our side,' Puccini said. 'Plus whatever number of police and Kaibiles the governor has bribed or scared into working for him.'

'Uruchurtu draws a lot of water in this town,' Marco said.

White dots appeared before my eyes, like the world was blistering with heat. My tongue ached for the stuff that was in the bottle with the snake, ached for that cutting brightness to slash me out of awareness, but all I could do was what I always did – wait out the sweats, try to appear normal.

'And the endgame of all of this?' I said. 'Because it seems a lot fucking bigger than family reunions all of a sudden.'

'The DEA wants Uruchurtu to stand trial,' Puccini said. 'And they want me as a witness.'

'Mightn't feel that way to you, cabrón,' Marco said, 'but this is how you be on the right side of history, know'm sayin?'

'What, because you're victims too?'

Puccini sat back, crossing his leg, and popped a grape into his mouth. The look in his eyes, I don't know, a building would have more pity if you were shot in front of it.

'Well, I wouldn't go that far,' he said. The skin of the grape popped between his teeth. 'But all of Urchurtu's victims, and all of our collected misjudgements, all our collateral damage, all of these will vanish with me if Uruchurtu is able to sink his own trial by sinking us.'

'Does this mean you're going to testify if I help you, then,' I said. 'Is that it?'

'Fuck no,' said Marco.

'We plan to carry out an operation against the governor,' said Puccini. 'An alternate trial, if you like, one that carries a heavier sentence than he would ordinarily face.'

'And who'll try you for what you've done?'

'Your conscience, I suppose.' Puccini pressed the tips of his fingers against his eyelids. 'But all of that will depend on your assistance.' He patted the iPad. 'Yes?'

My knuckles rapped the table. In my head I was on a hill-side outside Poza Rica, standing in the doorway of Julián Gallardo's house, handing his mother a Kleenex, a ten-metre tall refinery flame shimmering and roaring above our heads, and I was telling her how if I published his story, it wouldn't be justice, but it might be something like revenge, as if that might be a decent substitute.

'And I obviously haven't much of a choice here,' I said.

'Like I said, cabrón,' Marco said. 'We'll fuck you into a hole, and your friend, too.'

'Right.' I sighed, shaking my head. 'So, what's next?'

18

Forty minutes later I was sitting in a wooden booth at a pan-Asian restaurant, thinking how the little wooden protrusions around me looked like your photos of the shoreline pyramids that you'd seen from your year on the boat. Thai psychedelia from the '60s filtered out of the speakers, the red tassels of the lampshades swayed in the draught of the fans, and the air was a mellow buzz of chatter and rainbow fairy lights and things frying. The sweaty weight of the bulletproof vest I had on made my body feel like a swamp.

A woman who looked and acted like she was the owner of the place deposited a Christmas-red cocktail in front of me.

'Ah, don't worry about that,' I said, handing her back the cocktail.

'But it's free.'

'I know, I know. I just don't want one.'

She stood back a little. 'You ill?'

'Extremely.'

'Oh, well,' she said, and took a sip herself, before dropping a menu and walking away.

If she found the non-drinking annoying, the vegetarian-
ism was worse, but I negotiated myself a pad prik with tofu
swapped in for meat, then waited for the architect to show
up. Given how everything else had panned out for me the
last few days, it wasn't a surprise to see him push through
the doors just as I was blowing on my first forkful. He sat
four tables away, his back to me, and gulped down about half
of the complimentary cocktail when it arrived. From where
I was sitting, I could see him checking and rechecking his
OKCupid page, scrolling back up the chat, lingering over the
little blue squares that the messages flashed up in. He had a
smile playing around his mouth the whole time. Marco and
Puccini had really stuck the knife into him, however they'd
done it. He was going to be mightily pissed off, I thought to
myself, wiping my mouth and leaving the money clamped
under the rim of the dish I'd just cleared through, before getting to my feet and crossing the restaurant. As I was passing his
table, I turned, pointing at him.

'Hey,' I said, trying to sound puzzled. 'I *know* you, don't I?'

He looked up from his phone, his mouth a little open.

'From where?' he said.

'Yeah, yeah,' I said, wagging a finger at him. 'You're that
architect – Óscar Zappamundi, right? Read about one of your
projects in *Vogue*.' I pulled out a chair. 'You mind if I join you?'

'Well, yes, actually.'

'Great.' I pulled out a chair, sat down, and poured myself a
glass of water from the jug on his table.

He craned out of the booth, trying to get the owner's
attention.

'What are you going to tell them?' I said. 'That a bad man is making you scared?' I shook my head, lowering my voice. 'Look, I know you've got a date, I know you're looking forward to it, and I'm not going to keep you. Second she shows up, I'm out. OK?'

The man flushed.

'This is – this is really indiscreet, honestly.' He was muttering.

The owner walked towards our table.

'Everything OK here?'

'Just an espresso, if you would,' I said.

The architect looked at me, aghast, and said nothing.

'What?' I said. 'You can stretch to that, man, c'mon, you're Mr *Vogue*.' I sat back, crossed my legs. 'Anyway, like I was saying. Your name's not all I know about you. Where you work, for example.' Now I leaned forward onto the table, same as Marco had leaned towards me. 'And who you've worked for, too.'

That did it. The architect made to stand up.

'That's a really bad idea,' I said. My fist was in my jacket pocket. He saw the bulge. 'Now, c'mon.'

He stopped where he was and pressed the heels of his hands against his forehead.

'What do you want?' he said. 'Is it money?'

'Not money.' I slid a Krispy Kreme napkin across the table. 'Numbers. Twelve of them. The one for the gate. The one for the door. The one for the safe.'

'What?'

'For your office.' I rolled a pen towards him. 'C'mon. They're not going to know it was you. Get another of those cocktails down you and not even you'll remember.'

His bravado gave a last sputter.

'Or what?' He set his jaw at me.

The espresso arrived. The owner gave me a heavy look as she walked away.

'What do you fucking think?' I pushed the ramekin with the sugars in it across to him. 'Pour me in one, would you? I only have the one free hand.'

Shaking his head, he wrote down three four-digit codes and handed me the napkin.

'Top one's the front gate. Middle one's the door. Bottom one's the safe.'

'And?'

'And what?'

'And where's the safe?'

'Oh. Shit. Yes. Um, you just, you just go down through the building, all the way. Along the first floor. And you'll see a print of a Turner. It's behind that. The different plans, they're all on different hard drives, but they're labelled. You can't miss it.'

'Very good. And?'

His face was twisted with fear and frustration.

'And *what*?' His hands flapped the air.

My finger tapped the espresso cup.

'Jesus Christ.' He poured in the sugar.

'Much obliged.' I pocketed the napkin, drained my coffee, and gave him a pat on the shoulder as I left the booth.

19

A new, undamaged jeep swung up to the restaurant as I stepped out the door.

'All good, cabrón?' he said, as I climbed in.

'All good,' I said, and took my empty fist from the jacket pocket I'd said had the gun in it. I held up the Krispy Kreme napkin with the security codes on it.

'Excellent,' said Puccini from the back seat.

We pulled away from the kerb. Puccini handed a balaclava, a pair of black rubber gloves, and a ventilator mask through the gap between Marco's seat and mine. When I put the mask over my head, the ventilator sucked itself flush against my lips. The air through the mouthpiece tasted of swimming pool.

It was too late for anyone to be out – just cops and homeless people edging away from one another under the violet floodlights set up in front of the government buildings. Out of the Centro it was the same as every other poor neighbourhood, peeling concert flyers and MISSING posters, the faded paint of shopfronts, satellites and TV aerials and rebar poking up black against the light pollution.

Slowing through a junction there was a long, dragging moment where I saw an old man and a teenage boy kneeling in front of an indoor altar to Maximón. You'll see these altars all over Guatemala. Sometimes he's a soldier, sometimes he's an hacendado, sometimes he's a curandero, complete with flowing robes and gilt-edged paliacates. This one was an even mix of narco and priest, the light and smoke of the candles thick and billowing, a deep red that verged on purple, the man exhaling long garlands of tobaco puro smoke, the kid's mouth moving, his hands clasped over his mouth, the moustached statue looming above them, a shadow over his face from the brim of a cowboy hat, a cigarette smoking in the hole that had been drilled in to his mouth, his eyes upcast, pleading, the ceramic of his face gleaming sallow and feverish as the smoke crawled the glass covering his altar. Then Marco whipped the car around and the image snapped off the mirror, vanished into the night.

Inside the car we were quiet. It was just the scuba-diver gargle of mine and Puccini's ventilators, the hum of the engine, the rabbity tremor of the pulse in my throat.

Twenty minutes' drive took us to a neighbourhood of Spanish villas and out-of-place semi-Tudor houses, all lush hedgerows and razor-wire fences and pristine vintage letter-boxes. The big cold surges of fear pumping through me almost felt good, I was sweating that much.

Marco let Puccini and me out a couple of blocks from the architect's office. A car was parked right outside, the lights on, so Puccini took two flares from his belt and threw them hard against the front windows of the nearest car. Purple flames whooshed and crackled, blooming up against the seat. The alarms shrilled. The car outside the architect's office drove towards us, and, as it neared, Puccini shot out the windscreen, tossed a third flare into the smashed gap, and ran towards the car as the driver rolled, gagging, from the open door. Smoke billowed with a hiss into the air. By the time I got close enough, Puccini had knocked the driver out with a rabbit punch to the neck. The guy in the passenger seat was frozen in shock, his gun in his hand, but both hands up. When he saw me loom over him he dropped the pistol, then I said 'Sorry' and knocked him in the middle of the forehead with the butt of his dropped gun, unclicked his seatbelt and pulled him out of the car before it could catch fire.

His body crumpled into the road.

'Shit,' I said. 'Did I kill him?'

Puccini gave me a withering look, then sprinted for the gate, and I went after him, tapped in the code on the little panel, watched the metal doors clatter open before sliding through the gap. There weren't any sirens yet, but people were opening their doors up and down the lane, and I could hear raised voices. While Puccini covered me, I keyed in the code for the front door and moved through a conference room, all the way to the back of a space littered with desks and office chairs. My hip bumped a fire extinguisher to the ground as I ran.

The Turner print was hanging where the architect said it would be. Puccini lifted it from the wall and an alarm began to shrill.

'That fucker,' I said, but his code worked. The safe opened. Puccini lifted out the shoebox, tipped the hard-drives onto the floor, nudged through them with his toe, and grabbed the one with a label stuck to it that read 'LA FAENA'.

Feet stomped along the carpet, through the conference room, past the office space, and two dark shapes blurred into focus. My gun swung up, but I couldn't do it, it wasn't right, so I aimed at the fire-extinguisher, pulled the trigger, and felt the kick of the recoil as the white smoke went blooming up. Two men coughed and swore in the cloud. Puccini just shot them down, then grabbed me by the shoulder, pulled me to the side, and we ran for the window, but I didn't get more than ten paces before someone grabbed me by the ankle. A fist hit me in the face, the ventilator slid, cut the bridge of my nose, and the man yowled, missed me with a right hook, and I tried a left, got him in the groin with my first punch in about twelve years. Puccini's knee came up, then his gun came up, and there was a bang and the man dropped. Then something else hit me somewhere, probably the back of my head, it felt like, but it was hard to tell where – everything had gone very swimmy. Puccini's feet were getting further away. So was the room. The pain burst then, a blast that sent me sailing out across a black sea, and then a jet of fire carried me away entirely.

20

The pain woke me. It made me want to cry. I was lying down, bumping along in the back of a car that smelled of fear-sweat and mint chewing-gum. Marco was the driver. In the footwell where I was lying I saw packs of blood and a wrapped-up drip-tube with a capped syringe on the end. Streetlights whitened the inside of the car. The glare hurt, so I reached for one of those blood-packs and put it behind my head as a pillow.

Marco caught my eye in the rear-view mirror.

'You're OK, cabrón,' he said. His voice was all breezy calm, like a paramedic.

'Where's the boss?' I said.

Red and purple lights wobbled in jellyfish shapes past the window, resolving into letters, into the signs of a mall, then dimming as we dropped down an underpass.

'Divide and conquer.'

'What?' I sat up, put on my belt, and a big pain shunted like a bowling-ball from one side of my head to the other. 'What's that meant to mean?'

'Calm down, cabrón,' Marco said, and he was about to say more, I think, but then a sharp, unechoing crack smashed the window on his side, jolted him in the seat, and blood jetted across my face. Another two shots struck him, one in the shoulder, to go by his spin across the front passenger seat, another in the gut, to go by the smell. The jeep fishtailed, spun, crumpled to a halt against the inside wall of the tunnel, Marco's foot crammed against the accelerator, the tyres shrieking as they spun, dust rolling in a cloud over us, sticking to the blood on my face.

Each of the three holes in Marco was the size of a tomato and ringed with a divot of wet matter. The crotch of his jeans darkened. He was still kicking a little, like someone in a panic dream, and his little grunted sobs were a sleeper's, too.

How long that noise and movement went on for can't have been more than ten minutes on the clock, because that's as long as it takes for your lungs to fill with enough blood to drown you, but how long it felt to his smothering brain, as those ion transports and synapses and circuits futzed out, as all those flickers of burned-in memories and flukes of recollection rose up and dissolved, well, I don't know, it could have felt like hours, days, years. Part of me hoped it did feel that long. The rest of me hoped he saw and felt nothing at all.

It's like I told you before – death has a dozen smells, and Marco's was the same as the first one I'd witnessed, so far back and in such a blurry time of my life that I hadn't thought about it in years, had barely even thought of it as the first death I'd seen with my own two eyes, even though it must have been. Back when I'd been sleeping rough behind Taxqueña Metro, a homeless guy had freaked out, stabbed a cop, gotten shot in the ass, the bullet exiting through his balls, the spatter of burnt tubes like black pasta. The cops only called one ambulance, for their guy, left the homeless guy to crawl around and bawl and leave a long drag-mark of shit and blood across the concrete. He'd slumped down beside me at one point, asked for a cigarette, and I'd lifted it back and forth to his mouth while piss and blood darkened his pants, holding his hand for him. Since he'd been drunk when he'd attacked the cop, pain and booze and terror had him fluttering in and out of a sleep that slowly turned to death, and I'd had to finish the cigarette for him.

All I could do for Marco was what I'd done for the homeless guy – hold his hand, mutter nice things to him like he was a sick kid, listen as his breath became the thick gargle of a fucked soda fountain, feel the last crackle of motor response shut his fingers around mine, feel those fingers go cool in my grip.

Headlights washed over the jeep from behind. A cop-car slowed up.

First one car-door opened, then another. Before they could see me, I slit open one blood-pack with my keys, smeared the thick, metal-smelling goop over my face and neck, then took my pistol from the back of my pants, held a second blood-pack flush against the inside lining of my jacket, the muzzle of the pistol against the blood pack, and pulled the trigger, so they'd think I'd shot myself.

There was a bang. My ears rang. The blood-pack melted. A white heat seared the back of my hand, and I dropped forward against the square outline of the headrest of the seat in front of me, upflung blood dripping in strings from my cheek, my forehead pressed to the headrest, biting the inside of the mask to keep back my scream, so hard that I thought my canines would burst. The gun dropped from my hand. A smell of burned hair and cloth and plastic cut the fug of blood in the car.

In the rear-view, I saw the two cops duck, saw the one in the uniform throw his hands over his head. The one wearing a tie drew his gun.

Smoke trailed between my fingers. I tried to pretend I was back in Ireland, pheasant-hunting, playing dead under a hide of leaves, keeping my breaths small so my chest wouldn't move, counting back from forty, thirty-nine, thirty-eight, thirty-seven, my gaze blank, my eyes aimed at the still point of the jeep's radio-dial, my eyelids trembling with the held-back wish to blink.

'Relájate. Carajoo,' said the man wearing a tie, his voice a slow, Campeche drawl, and the chill that ran through me, hearing that voice, it was colder than the shock I'd felt watching Marco's head crack back with the impact of the shot, because this guy, even though he'd pulled up in a cop-car, I knew him as a former associate of Marco's. He'd flung me to the ground of a safehouse and through the shards of a man's blown-off head, and he'd kicked me in the ribs while the blood and brains dripped down my face. Now, though, he must be working for the governor.

'I know Marco,' Mangueras said, his outline growing clearer in the wing mirror – sleepy-eyed, curly-haired, his walk slow and rolling. Last time I'd seen him, he'd clouted me across the jaw with a pistol, pulled a bag over my head. 'He hates jail cells.'

'You want to make sure?' the cop behind him said. He was skinny, about forty, his hair slicked back, his moustache thin. 'Just in case?'

Mangueras tutted and said, 'No, man, both dead as fuck.'

'The other one, too?' said the cop.

In my head, I was seventeen, under a leaf-hide in the old quarry behind my parents' house, waiting for a pheasant to rise, feathers clapping, from the back hedge, the air tasting of loam and chlorophyll, instead of the swimming-pool tang of the ventilator.

'Well?' said the cop.

'He's got a hole in him,' said Mangueras, 'and there's smoke and blood coming out of the hole. You want to put a finger in?'

'Takes as long to shoot him as it does to say all that, chief.'

'Hey,' said Mangueras. 'Who's paying who here?'

'Sorry, chief. Hey, you know who he is?'

'He's dead, who gives a shit.'

'OK, chief.'

'Doubting fucking Thomas.' Mangueras reached through the window, tinkling the broken glass. He turned the key off in the ignition. The squalling of the tyres stopped. 'I swear to God. This country.'

There was the sound of him clapping Marco on his neck, and he said, 'I'm sorry, brother.'

124

'Chief?' said the cop from behind him. 'All OK?'

'Shut the fuck up.' Mangueras' arm drew back, and he took a long, wadded rag out of the pocket of his shirt, opened the door of the jeep, and pulled Marco's body upright in the seat. Blood splashed across his shoes. 'Ah, fuck.'

From the other pocket, he took out a roll of tape, pulled off two strips with his teeth, and stuck Marco's hands to his shoulders, before stuffing one end of the rag into his mouth. My heart beat in my teeth. The cop with the slicked-back hair approached with a bottle of what smelled like petrol, soaked the end of the rag, then stuffed it into Marco's mouth. Mangueras took out a lighter, lit the rag, and there was a deep *thoom* and a blue flame licked along Marco's chest, as far as his mouth. The heat washed over my face but I didn't move, even though I could smell the ends of my hair singeing.

Mangueras raised a hand against the heat. The cop sprang back.

'Adiós, carnal,' Mangueras said, and saluted the body.

Marco's beard flared. His cheeks began to sputter, to hiss. My breath was going fast now, watching the cop and Mangueras climb back in the car. Marco's entire head caught fire. Even through the ventilator, the waves of burn-smell kept washing over me. A flame dripped from the upholstery of his side to the headrest on mine, and I felt the mask begin to heat up against my face.

'Oh, hurry *up*,' I said to the reflection of the car in the rear-view mirror.

The lights went on. The car reversed, turned.

The flame on the headrest grew, widened, closing towards my face. The rubber and glass of the ventilator were heating up, burning my forehead, my cheeks.

'For fuck's sake,' I said through my teeth.

The car rose out of sight, I opened the door, and dropped out of the car, sucking in air like I'd been underwater, dragging my satchel with me, and scrabbled hand over hand across the floor of the tunnel before the rest of the jeep went up.

Vein-shaped spills of petrol leaked from the bonnet of the crumpled jeep. Thick swags of black smoke rose from Marco's body. The burn on my hand was a sizzled purple the shape of a lipstick kiss. Dousing it with water from my flask made it worse, but I didn't have time to yowl about it for too long, because another set of police-lights came washing over me from the far end of the tunnel, and I groaned and dropped my head and my gun to the ground.

The car braked. Doors opened and shut. Two cops got out, a man and a woman. Even with my head resting on my forearms I was able to get a good look at them. He had black hair gelled into little spikes like a '90s footballer, wearing a leather jacket over a shirt and skinny tie, black slacks, and knackered loafers. He looked about a year older than me. The other cop must have had about a decade on both of us, but her pantsuit was in better nick than his, and she looked a good bit healthier than either he or I could hope to.

The man whistled, said, 'Car looks like a Coke can.'

'Yes,' said the woman.

'As in, like, a crushed one,' said the man.

'I guessed that,' she said.

'Do I call an ambulance?' said the man.

'Not yet,' she said. 'The radio is being weird.'

The metal of the jeep I'd been in was ticking with heat, faster and faster, like a little clock counting down.

'Hey, there's another body!' the man shouted. 'Stay down! Drop your gun!'

'He's already done that,' the woman said. She sounded tired. They must have spent a lot of time in that car together. She walked towards me, kicked the gun out of reach, pressed the sole of a steel-toe-capped boot against my burned wrist.

'You know your rights?' she said to me.

'More or less,' I said.

'Well, you don't have any here,' she said. Handcuffs jangled. Her knee pinned me to the ground.

A yell cut the air outside, far up the slope to the entrance. The two police crouched, their guns drawn. The yell became a pleading voice, but then a rifle cracked and the pleas stopped.

'What the hell?' the male cop said.

The tick of the car was a rattle now, and there was a deep boom that I felt with my body. Metal clattered. Glass smashed. The cops swore. I flinched into a tighter curl on the ground. The blast lifted the jeep into the air and then it crunched back down onto its axles.

'Oh, God, that smells terrible,' the man groaned. Then I heard him shout, 'Hands up!' again, heard his feet slide on the ground, heard him draw a gun.

'David,' the woman said, yanking my arm upwards, to cuff my other arm. 'I have this one.'

'I'm not talking to him,' David hissed. 'Look!'

The woman let go of the chain around my wrists.

'Jesus,' she said.

'On your knees!' the man shouted.

'You know who that is?' the woman said.

The tone of her voice sent the relief leaking through me like iced water. Turning my head, I saw Puccini kneeling on the floor of the tunnel, the headlights of the Crossfox throwing his shadow over me. Blood ran down the seam in his face. The look in his eyes made me think of a fox caught in a snare.

'Oh my God,' the male cop said, and started running towards Puccini.

'Wait!' said his partner. Her knee rose from my back. 'Let me.'

The male cop shook the cuffs from his belt, but he was too slow. His gun dipped for a second, and that was all that Puccini needed to spring forward, knocking the male cop to the ground. His fist slammed the cop's wrist, the pistol fell from his grip, and then Puccini had him hauled upright, the muzzle pressed to his neck.

'Alright, alright,' the cop pinning me said, lowering her gun. 'What do you want?'

The male cop struggled in Puccini's grip, but Puccini just lifted the stock of the gun and smacked him in the temple with it.

'My daughter,' Puccini said. His voice was nearly a sob. It made me sick to hear, sick and afraid. 'Just my daughter. Just let me see her.' He started dragging the unconscious cop towards us. The gun hung from his hand. His movements looked all baggy and awkward.

'Just to see her,' he said. 'Even if it's through a window. Just to know she's safe. To know where she'll be.'

The detective took a step back.

'If you put down the gun,' she said, 'we can help you.'

'OK,' said Puccini. He took a deep breath, lifted both his hands, and let the gun drop. 'OK.'

'Alright,' the woman detective began to say, but then a pair of handcuffs whipped up from Puccini's hand, lassoed her gun, flipped it to the ground. Before she could react, Puccini shoved the inert body of her partner at her and knocked them both on the ground.

'Right,' Puccini said, and collected his pistol. His body language was back to normal again, his voice back to scary again. 'Keys.'

'In my pocket,' the woman cop said.

Puccini kneeled beside me and undid the cuffs, then handed me back my gun, before slapping my cuffs on her wrists instead.

'I'm sorry about Marco,' I said.

He looked at the smoke, at the body, at the blazing wreck of the jeep. His mouth became a crease. He shook his head.

'He did well,' Puccini said, then looked down at the woman cop, reached into his pocket, and dropped an ID card beside her.

'I shot this man outside the tunnel,' he said. 'You know him?'

'Not well,' she said, her head turned sideways to look, 'but he's in homicide. Our division.'

'That colleague of yours,' he said, 'was working for the former governor of Veracruz. He was coming to finish the job.'

'What job?'

'Killing my colleague,' said Puccini, 'and then killing you. He knew you were here because he was monitoring your radio.'

'And how do you know that?'

Puccini pressed a finger and his thumb to his eyelids.

'Because I was monitoring his radio,' he said. 'After I killed him, the mic was still squawking. Sergeant from a city-centre precinct, asking if the people matching your and your part-ner's descriptions "had been stalled".'

The cop looked at the ID, frowning. Then she looked up at Puccini.

'Look, we don't have anything to do with you, or this governor, or anyone,' she said. 'We're homicide. We just happened to be nearby, answered a radio-call about the gun-shots. That's all. Honestly. You let us go, you won't hear a thing about us again. We didn't know anything before, so we can forget all about it now. It's just a coincidence.'

'You've already seen too much,' said Puccini. 'And I need more numbers. So you either work for me, or I leave you to them.'

She thought for a minute, her tongue pressing against the wall of her cheek.

'The radio has been funny all day,' she said. 'We called for an ambulance earlier. They said they were aware of the fire in the tunnel.' She gave a backward nod at the jeep. 'But that thing hadn't even blown up yet.'

'You can't trust your own people any more,' said Puccini. 'The only people who can help you are my colleague and I.'

She turned a hard look on me.

'And what's he?' she scoffed. 'The intern?'

'Harsh,' I said.

'Have you made your choice?' Puccini said.

'What choice?' said the cop. 'Lift him off me.'

Puccini and I stooped. He took the male cop by the shoulders, and I took him by the ankles. He was breathing like he was asleep. Puccini opened the boot with one hand and laid the cop head-first inside.

'He won't suffocate in here?' I said, lowering the cop's feet into the boot. He stirred a little, grunted, and gave a little cough.

'Probably not,' his partner said. 'He keeps suspects in there all the time.'

'A joy to work with,' I said, and slammed the boot. The cop inside sat up with a cry, smacked his head, and began to beat the inside of the metal. Puccini looked at me, shaking his head, then walked to the driver door, opened it, and leaned through. There was a crack of plastic and the sound of wires being yanked out, then Puccini dropped the mess that remained of their police-radio to the ground.

'Right,' Puccini said, opening the rear door. 'In.'

The detective did as he said, then Puccini shut the door and climbed into the driver's seat. I got in beside him, the muscles of my legs feeling as bockety as old bedsprings.

A helicopter thrummed not far off, close enough for the draught of its rotors to suck up trash and dust. A white floodlight swung back and forth beyond the mouth of the tunnel. Muffled cries and thuds shook the back of the car.

'Shut the fuck up, David,' said the cop, elbowing the seat. 'We're OK. Try to relax.'

'*Relax?*' David screamed through the boot.

Puccini drove off. Marco's jeep was dying to a smoulder behind us, its smoke chasing our car, filling the mouth of the tunnel, as everything Marco had ever been – his head, his body, his voice, his thoughts of his wife, his memories of the desert – petered out into nowhere.

21

Back at the safehouse, we got David's colleague to open the boot. It didn't seem to calm him down very much to see her, but he'd probably have ripped mine or Puccini's throat out with his teeth if it had been us. He flopped onto the ground, gasping.

'What the fuck, Sandra?' he said.

'Please, come in,' Puccini said. He'd opened the front door. 'There's food. Things to drink.'

David looked up at Sandra. She just jerked her head towards the door and walked in. Maya was sitting at the kitchen island with a bottle of beer and her laptop.

'What the hell happened to your face?' she said when she saw me. 'Jesus. Shouldn't you be in a hospital?'

'What?' I touched my forehead. My fingers came away wet. 'Oh. It's not mine.'

She looked at me for a moment.

'Wait,' she said. 'Where's the other guy? Marco.'

Puccini was acting like he hadn't heard.

'Make yourselves at home,' he said, and shook drops of condensation from the lids covering the trays, then began loading plates from the spread on the table. 'It shouldn't be too stale.'

'Maya, these are our new associates,' Puccini said as the two cops entered the kitchen.

She looked the newcomers over.

'You cops?' she said.

'Homicide detectives, actually.' David fixed his shirt and skinny tie.

'Right.' Maya shut her laptop and picked up her beer. 'Goodnight.' She headbutted my shoulder on her way past, but gently. 'I'm glad you're alive.'

'Ah, but for how long?' I said, as I walked to the fridge.

The beers looked less tempting than they had earlier. Maybe it was the adrenal buzz in my body, doing more of what the drink had always done for me. After draining a small carton of juice, I brought three bottles to the table and popped the caps off.

'If I may.' Puccini handed a plate each to the cops. David looked at Sandra, as if waiting for a signal.

'You want me to feed you, is that it?' She sat down at the kitchen island.

'Wonderful,' Puccini said. 'Now, we're going to need to divide and conquer here, if you don't mind.'

'What?' David said, around a mouthful of ciabatta and brie.

'Well, we have two separate concerns,' Puccini said. 'The first is the security of my daughter. We can guarantee that easily – Maya, the colleague whom you just met, she will be interviewing her tomorrow at her whereabouts, raising awareness of our family's plight, of the dangers of police laxity in dealing with the threat of the fleeing governor, et cetera, et cetera.' His hand circled in the air. 'This being a women's shelter, I believe Sandra might be best assigned to that. We have a slight transport issue, having only one vehicle, but you can find secure arrangements, I'm sure.'

'You're taking our car, then,' Sandra said. She shook her head. 'I've never even lost a badge before this.'

'What's my job then?' David said.

'Well.' Puccini placed his hands together, his fingers steepled. 'The closer I am to my daughter, the more danger she's in. And I don't expect you to put up much resistance if they catch you.' He raised a hand. 'No offence.

'No – the only way to be safe,' he continued, loading a ciabatta with ham and cheese, 'is if they are all stopped.'

David's bottle of beer stopped halfway to his mouth.

'So we find the governor and arrest him?' he said. 'Is that it?'

'I had another idea,' said Puccini, and shrugged. 'But, well, let the best idea win. Now, tomorrow we liaise with an associate. He has most of the equipment – if none of the manpower – that we require. I will also need to go to a Walmart.'

David made a face.

'Walmart?' he said.

'Yes.'

David shrugged.

'Well, if you're sure. Fuck it, why not.' He sat back on the stool. 'Cheers to that.' He took a long drink.

'What, just like that?' Sandra said.

'Uh, yeah?' he said. 'The biggest arrest of the decade, that's got to be.'

'Well, then,' said Puccini. 'Take some rest now. You can sleep on the couch. I only ask that you give me your phones.'

David looked at Sandra.

'Just do it,' she said, and handed hers over.

'Thank you,' Puccini said, taking both the phones, before reaching for the knife-block, sliding out a mallet, and dashing the phones to pieces against the kitchen island. David tried to protest for a second, but Sandra just watched like she'd been expecting it.

'This will be factored into your compensation,' Puccini said, and replaced the mallet. He drained his beer and got off the stool. 'Now, if you'll excuse me, I think some rest would be advised.' He took four pairs of handcuffs from his belt. I left the room before he bound them up. I'd seen enough.

22

Upstairs, Maya was in my room, face down, in a starfish shape that took up most of the bed.

'Are you serious?' I said.

She lifted her head from the pillow.

'You think I'm sleeping on my own in this place?' She curled up. 'Put a chair by the door or something. And you fucking stink, my God, what is that? Open a window.'

Through the glass I saw orange bales of smoke rolling through the light pollution. 'It's probably worse out there.' I sat down on the bed, my legs suddenly heavy with tiredness, while pictures of the day – the schoolkid we'd nearly run down, and his little sky-blue fisherman's cap, Marco's body kicking in the seat, the crackling violet jets of Puccini's flares – streamed so fast that I knew that trying to sleep would be pointless.

'What happened out there?' Maya said quietly.

'Ah, you don't want to know.' My hoodie was saturated with diesel-smoke, flare-smoke, Marco's particles, and I let it drop to the floor.

'That bad?'

'Yup.'

'Shit.' She sat up, propped on the pillows. 'I can't drop off either. Like, I saw someone die today, you know?'

'What? Who?'

'That car. You know. The one that crashed.'

'Eh.'

Maya bit her thumbnail. 'It's like, bodies, those I can handle, yeah? But when it's real-time?' She shook her head.

'You'll get a hell of a book out of this,' I said. 'That's for sure.'

Maya pulled a face, then said, 'I don't know if I want to. I don't know how you're so OK with everything.'

'I don't know. I suppose blind fucking terror gets pretty educational after a while.' I lay back down. My eyes hurt, and the back of my hand stung – from the burn, from the broken glass of the other night, the two kinds of pain were blurring together. 'Pure as the kerbside guck. But this is the only way the governor pays for anything, you know. Like, Puccini, he's actually the good guy here. Kind of.'

'Quelquefois je suis bon diable,' Maya said, her hands behind her head, looking up at the ceiling. 'The whole thing, it reminds me of that.'

'What?'

'Baudelaire.' She frowned at me. 'C'mon, man, you're the one went to a posh university, yeah?'

'I studied engineering. What's the quote?'

'You have me on the spot now.' She sighed. 'But OK, so, strictly off the top of my head, yeah? This guy's sitting in a really shitty restaurant, eating the worst soup in the world, when he notices this guy sitting next to him, giving him these big sad eyes like the cat from *Shrek*, yeah?'

Carlos' wide, needy eyes in the Parque Delta Chinese restaurant, on the morning I'd collected him after his run-in at the bar, lit up inside my head again.

'And the guy's reaching for his wallet,' Maya said, 'about to give the man watching him something, because he thinks he's a beggar, but then the guy watching him introduces himself, says he's the Devil, says sorry for taking his table, it's just there's none left. And this devil, he's a shabby guy, pretty pitiful, and the narrator's about to lose his mind, because even though he's the Devil, he's really fucking annoying, too, yeah? And our guy, all he wants is to get on with his shitty soup. But whatever, the Devil's not having it, and he won't be paid off, he just wants to talk, which is worse, you know? And so the narrator, he finally works up the balls to say, "Look, my soup is getting cold, could you leave me alone? I'm tired of hearing about all the stuff you feel guilty about." And then the Devil gets offended, all pissy, sits back, fiddling with his tie, and he pays the guy's bill, gets up to leave, says, in this full-on "Let-me-speak-to-the-manager" voice, yeah? He says, "Monsieur, quelquefois je suis bon diable".'

'And that means?'

'"Sometimes I'm one of the good ones",' she said. 'More or less.'

'The international motto of cops and journalists.' The knot in my back wasn't the kind stretching could do anything about. I sat up, knuckling my eyes, my head all spiky inside with the

139

memory of this story I'd done about organ trafficking, when I'd interviewed some gang members who had seemed OK enough or at least low-level enough for it to feel safe to go back to their safehouse, to see if I could get better pictures, better video, better words, but, when I'd got there, I don't know, it had been like a nightmare – stacks of cling-wrapped heroin on the safehouse table, a girl lying comatose on a mattress in the back room, a drip in her arm, a paper sheet over her, an EKG machine and an ice-loaded Oxxo beer-cooler beside her, the air loud with banda and heart-monitor beeps, and strong with the smell of dirty feathers, burnt hair, silverfish, while a heavy guy eased the door shut with his knee before I could peer deeper into the murk of that room, the tape recorder ticking on and on, until I'd gotten too drunk and high to do anything else but slither into the corner with a tequila bottle and wait out the spins, drinking until I was no longer able to hear what he and the heavyset guy were doing to the girl.

My hands tangled in my hair, thinking of it all.

'Here, I need a walk.' I got to my feet. 'I'll be back in a bit. You want me to lock you in?'

'Nah.' Maya slumped back down on the bed. 'I'll just scream, blood-curdlingly, if I need you.'

23

Woozy with heat, my head a throbbing weight on my neck, I stood smoking on the balcony, watching the lights, foot tapping the tiles, the night shining like a split coal from the scrub fires beyond the pools and the villas on the hilltops – all of it looking too new for anything atrocious to have happened there, all of it really just a terraformed section of hell, of five hundred years of hell. The night felt too loud. My head hurt. I felt like the crickets were five centuries' worth of screaming ghosts, and I had to look away, because there was no escape anywhere, and found myself staring at the wreck of builders' rubble at the foot of the safehouse garden – ground-up chunks of tarmac and stone, wet black muck and gravel, the crater left by a canted-up eucalyptus tree, its huge nude roots straggling in the air – but I couldn't look at any of that too long before the lights around the balcony took on foggy coronas, began to hover and wander, and the hedges shook off their outlines, turned to green blobs, all of it too sudden for me to try that counting back from forty trick, my head too fried anyway to get past thirty-six before the din of the air – fire-crackle, cricket-shirr – got too loud to keep track, and so all I could do was crouch to my knees, the smoke I breathed out rising to join the clouds that drifted down from the fire on the hills, but lengthening, too, solidifying into legs, a torso, arms, into Carlos standing beside me on the balcony.

'Jesus,' he said, and took a step back. His shoulders were hunched, his look cagey. He was wearing the clothes he'd had on the last time I'd seen him, except the shirt had holes in it, and his jeans and trainers were caked with blood and shit. 'It's you.'

With one hand Carlos rubbed the collar of bruises around his neck. When he lifted the hand away I saw the red circle of a bullet-hole printed there. He took a cigarette from my packet, lighting up with a thin blue flame that appeared above one fingertip, then clapped a hand on my shoulder. The smell off him was atrocious, and my stomach heaved. I don't know how I must have looked on that balcony, pacing around, twisting my hands in my hair, muttering to myself.

Carlos laughed. Smoke puffed through the holes in his chest.

'What a reception, vato,' he said.

'Missing you is shit,' I managed to say, and I think he was about to say something else when the bullet-holes on his chest and head began to widen, his outline began to waver, and then he was gone, leaving me alone in a night that smelled of burning thorn-bush and mesquite. My legs wobbled and so did the balcony – side to side, like the world's slowest earthquake was happening.

The screen door opened. It was Puccini. He said something.

'What?'

'Panic attack.' He held a glass bottle of Coke out to me. 'You're having one.'

The lights throbbed. The backs of my hands were white with sweat.

'You're handling it well.' He was playing with the lid of a glass bottle of his own.

'Years of practice.' I sank forward onto the balcony. A mosquito whined above my head. 'You couldn't sleep either?' I said to him.

For a moment Puccini watched, then flicked the air. The whining stopped. A tiny body rattled across the tiles.

'I just don't sleep much,' he said. 'Habit.'

'Army?'

Puccini laughed and said, 'No, the sites. Carpenter has to be there first, always, my foreman said.'

'I see.' The sugar rush was killing the din in my head.

Puccini's eyes scanned the dark.

'You must be wondering,' he said, 'what you might get out of any of this.'

'I assumed being left alive was the pay bit.' There was a bin directly below the balcony, so I drained the Coke, dropped the bottle over the edge, watched it roll around the rim, drop with a hush into the bag, and clank against the metal bottom. 'Three points.'

Puccini hefted his bottle from one hand to the other.

'Staying alive isn't enough,' he said. He opened the flap of a pocket in his cargo-pants and handed me a Guatemalan passport. The photo inside was his, but the name wasn't.

'Biometric, right weight to the paper, everything like that,' he said.

'That contact in immigration is good.' I flicked through the pages. There were even blurry, back-dated stamps to make it look more real.

'We looked into your background,' he said. 'All the way back.'

My thumb stopped flicking the pages.

Love, if you get this, it's like I told you before – you can spend your whole life watching over people, easy. Back in Ireland, I'd been the guy who'd keep an eye out for teachers during lunchtime scuffles, and then hidden the booze nicked from parents' drinks cabinets, and then stowed my mates' weed and ecstasy stashes in my flat, and then, OK, so maybe one of those times had gone wrong on me.

'We can do you one for anywhere,' Puccini said. 'You can go back to who you were, to where you were, and leave you with the starter capital to make anything you want happen for you.

'You can step out of who you are,' said Puccini. 'You can be nowhere.'

The pictures hit me like a rush of iced water – Helen, Callum, and me on the campus of our university, sat under an umbrella while snow came down over the Rose Garden, passing the Sancerre back and forth, a fine lace of bubbles sliding down the neck and breaking past the shoulder of the bottle. Just to stay with them, to stay surrounded by all those bright lives as they went trampolining on to bigger and better things than I could have imagined – I'd have done anything to make that happen. In the end, I had done almost anything to make it happen, and it had blown up in my face, and that knowledge brought on a second rush of images that made my chest ache – the neat sweep of Helen's bobbed haircut, just brushing her shoulders, the laptop glowing blue in the lenses of her horn-rims, the rattle of her fingers on the keys, tapping in her father's credit-card details, buying us our flights to Mexico.

The passport caught the light. All those memories, all those hurts, all those people whose pain I'd written up and profited from, all those spikes that no drink could numb me to, that no programme had ever been able to pull out – they could be gone if I wanted. I whacked the passport against my hand. This was a way to disappear without it looking like I'd wanted to vanish. This was a way to die but leave no body. This was how to be nowhere, and all I had to do was obey.

Puccini held out his hand for the passport, slipped it back into his pocket.

'Nobody coming after you, ever again,' he said.

'Except for you.'

He shrugged.

The night crackled. My fingers flexed on the balcony rail.

Puccini peered into his bottle, took a long drink.

'And you couldn't find anybody else for this?' I said. 'Nobody you could threaten? Nobody you could bribe?'

Puccini shook his head.

'This late in things?' he said. 'So many are dead. So many are in jail. So many are broken in other ways. It's been a long road, and they hunt you all the way, and if the future doesn't get you, your history will.'

Crickets and chicharras clicked and shirred. For a second, we said nothing, but then Puccini went rigid where he stood and he drew his arm back like a shot-putter, the bottle flying from his hand in a clean arc, streaming brownish fizz through the air, and a shape dressed head to toe in black prowling by the gable end uttered a cry and toppled as the bottle clunked him square in the temple, and his gun dropped from his hand, jerking on the telephone-cord clipping it to his belt.

Behind us, the lights blinked off and an alarm beeped. The sizzle of the wire fences fell silent.

'Go downstairs,' Puccini hissed, and climbed the balcony rail. 'Clear the house. Clear the gulley around the house. Go.' He dropped onto the roof one level down, and I heard his breath go in hard, saw him pull a face like something hurt, but he righted himself, jumped to the grass. The bottle hissed in circles, propelled by jets of fizz. The gunman's ankle twitched. The jet from the bottle died to a glug and Puccini grabbed it, smashed its base against the ground, then stabbed the man lying there again and again in the neck. The man on the ground coughed out a load of ragged vowels that almost sounded like words, but he stopped after the fifth jab of the smashed bottle.

'What are you waiting for?' Puccini hissed, and waved at me, and I sprinted inside, making straight for the stairs.

From below, I heard a deep click. The front door swung open. A gun-barrel nosed through the gap.

So I pushed through.

Love, if you get this, I didn't want to do it, I swear. Something else in me swung the gun up, a current of cold water, it felt like, just washing my arm into motion, so that my finger squeezed the trigger of its own accord, with nothing I could call by my own name making that motion happen.

There was more than one bang. For a second I thought I'd missed, that he was shooting back at me, and I dropped and pressed myself to the wall, but then the rattle of gunfire stopped, and I could hear somebody sobbing a little, could hear them fall to the carpet, and I poked my head out, saw a masked gunman dressed head to toe in black holding the stub of his wrist and falling onto the floor, because my shot had struck the magazine of his pistol and blown up every cartridge inside. He rolled. His chest was a mess, his neck, too, but I kept the gun on him as I stepped down to the ground floor. The gun was lighter and warmer in my hand now that I'd fired it, but its black shine was still surreal to me, so close to a movie version of itself that for a moment I was sure I was holding a toy.

The man I'd shot was still moving when I got there, his remaining hand moving in the air as if he was stroking someone's face. Through the holes in his balaclava I could see a wet fog spreading through his eyes. When I lifted his head, a whole lot of blood and some sort of muttering about Jesus spilled from his mouth, then he shivered and stopped moving, the back of his head already cooling.

Appliances beeped, lights blinked, and I could hear the cops struggling on the couches Puccini had led them to. When they saw me, David yelled against his gag. I was the only person moving through the house, jerking around the corners, the sweat on my hands making the gun slippery, sure I was doing everything wrong, sure that any second there'd be a bang, sure that I'd try to turn but find myself falling through a darkness that had no floor.

Outside, there was still nothing – just Puccini checking the area around the man he'd stabbed. His steps were as delicate as a cat's. He turned his back for one second, a black shape poured out of the shadows nearest him, above where I stood in the concrete gulley between the house wall and the start of the grass, and I hooked an arm around the shadow's ankle and pulled. The man spun, kicked me in the face and sent me sprawling, but Puccini just turned and shot him twice in the back. Blood fountained all over my head.

'Ah, Christ,' I shouted.

'Shut up,' Puccini said, turning the body with his foot. He aimed at the man's face and pulled the trigger again. 'Did you clear the house?'

'All OK,' I said. 'I think.'

'Right. Get your friend.'

When I went back through the house, I saw the man I'd killed lying where I'd left him, his blood a round mirror of my face. The sight of it made my stomach kick once, hard, but no vomit came up, just shivers all over. Upstairs, I tried the door to Maya's room, but she'd locked it.

'It's me,' I said.

She said nothing, but I heard her move across the floor, heard the lock click. She opened the door a little.

She was holding the bedside lamp like it was a club.

'You should maybe unplug that thing,' I said.

'Fuck off.' She dropped the lamp, pointed at the streaks of blood on the knees of my jeans, on my face, on my hoodie. 'And that's whose, this time?'

'Pass me my bag.'

From downstairs, I could hear Puccini undoing the cops' cuffs. He spoke in a low voice. David did not.

'What the fuck, man?' he yelled. 'We could have helped you.'

'I do not want to go down there,' Maya said, as we took the first steps downstairs.

'At least you don't have to be in a car with the guy.'

Puccini was carrying two black sports-bags through the hall. He'd been gone for a couple of minutes. I watched him step across the pool of blood and exploded cartridges on the carpet and doormat.

'Our transport issues have been solved,' Puccini said. 'The attackers left their jeep.' Then he continued up the driveway, where he slid back the electric gates with one hand.

The cops, Maya, and I all stared.

'Right,' Sandra said to David. 'Be safe out there.'

'Will do.' He fixed his tie, looking bashful, and poked at the carpet with the toe of his loafer, then Puccini whistled from the drive, and he left through the open door with a wave and a muttered 'Mucho gusto' to Maya.

Sandra gave me a hard look and walked through to the kitchen.

'Coffee?' she said to Maya.

'Oh, yes, please.'

'I'll leave you to your new best friend,' I said, and gave Maya a hug, then let go, scratching the back of my neck. 'I'll be off, so.'

'Don't let him make you do anything fucked up.' She head-butted me on the shoulder, harder this time. 'And be careful.'

Puccini was standing next to the driver-door of a black Dodge RAM, smoking a cigarette and frisbeeing the jeep's front and back licence plates into the privet hedge.

'Ah, don't worry,' I said. 'The white guy never dies at the end of these things.'

She made a face.

'Lately,' she said, 'I'm thinking bets on that kind of thing look increasingly off.'

Puccini whistled again from the driveway. An engine turned over. Headlights flashed.

'Right so.' I squeezed her shoulder. 'Bye, now.'

I walked up the drive. Puccini had shifted to the passenger seat and was holding the driver door open for me. David was sitting in the back seat, checking the mechanism of the pump-action shotgun that Marco had handed me the day before.

'Guess this must feel pretty unusual to you, huh?' David said to me.

'I wish,' I said, and turned the car around.

The hillside fires glowed orange in the rear-view as I took us careering down the slope towards the highway out of the city. A smooth wash of adrenaline and relief beat in me, stronger than any tide. Once again I'd gotten through. Once again I hadn't been shot or hurt. There was no point thinking how long either of those things would be true. Puccini reached across my lap, pressed a switch under the dash, and our siren started to waul and flash as we sped into the night, the city vanishing behind us, lost to the billowing smoke.

24

We didn't stop driving until it was bright, swapping from me to David to Puccini and back every hour or so. We were nearing a petrol station somewhere above Xela, heading towards the highlands, when Puccini said, 'I'm going to need you to pull over.'

David was at the wheel.

'Gauge looks OK to me,' he said. 'More than half full.'

'Pull over,' Puccini said.

David shrugged and did as he was told.

Apart from a dented Ford pickup ours was the only vehicle on the petrol-station forecourt. The air was a high blue above the curving walls of rock that the highway had been cut through.

'You keep an eye out,' said David, slamming the door. 'I'm going to the bathroom.'

'Sure.' I yawned, and started to fill up. My bones hummed from the long drive.

'He's a very earnest young man,' Puccini said, watching David saunter across the forecourt. 'That could work against him.'

'I feel like he has watched even more bad films than I have,' I said.

'Yes. Let me go buy some coffee,' Puccini said. He walked towards the shop.

While I let petrol glug into the tank, I looked over at the field beside the forecourt, watching an older woman as she picked her way across burned-looking stooks that were caught all over with burger-shells and sweet-wrappers. She had on a floral dress and a faded JIMMY MORALES PRESIDENTE baseball cap. The pylons above her head were rusted, the wires had been repaired so many times that they looked like vines. A large orange iguana scrabbled out from between two furrows, a corn-leaf in its mouth, and she swiped at the thing with a hoe until it was out of range.

While I was yawning, stretching, and picking at the paper-fine blisters of sunburn on my forearm, I felt somebody walk up behind me – a beggar, I figured – and was turning to say, 'I don't have change', but a hand spun me around, a fist popped me in the spleen, and I dropped, winded, to my knees. The guy was tall and heavyset and had a broken nose. His elbow hit my jaw so hard that the cap on my incisor broke off, skittered across the concrete. A second pair of hands clapped over my ears. The feathery boom made my head ring. The light went cloudy, my head jerked back, and the next breath I took sucked the inside wall of a plastic bag into my mouth, flapping against the palate. For a second everything went clear, as the inhale drew the bag taut against my eyes. My hand clawed out behind me, clamped shut around the bag guy's ball-sack, my thumb jammed under the shaft of his dick, and I twisted, hard, and tissues ripped with a grunt that I could feel, and the guy yowled, so I tugged harder, twisted, and I heard my neck crick as he tugged the bag over my head harder again.

Through the bag, I saw the fogged shape of a cosh fall towards my temple, and I let go of the guy's ball-bag, threw up my hands to shield my face, but then there was a light thud and a spatter of liquid, someone bawled, the cosh dropped back, and I saw steam rising between the fingers of the man who'd been holding it. The air was sharp with the smell of coffee and superheated jelly. The man had his hands over his eyes. A gun went off. The bag went loose. A plume of red rose and vanished. Another shot cut off the bawling. Turning, I saw the guy who'd grabbed me take a shaky step backwards, his tongue lolling in the gap where his chin had been. Another shot sent flecks of his skull stinging across my cheek. Scattered bone tinked against the Magna pump. He fell, and I saw Puccini standing outside the petrol-station shop, a pistol in one hand, a tray with one remaining coffee in the other.

The driver of the pickup came galloping out of the shop, his flip-flops going *whap-whap-whap* across the forecourt, and cars honked on the road, just beyond the petrol-station exit. Looking up, I saw a matt-black Toyota Camry come barrelling out of a blind curve, making for the exit ramp, a guy with a crew-cut leaning out the passenger window, his submachine gun levelled at Puccini, but the pickup was shrieking off the forecourt, and it clattered into the Camry, knocked off the front bumper, knocked the guy's gunfire off target, and puffs of white dust shot up where Puccini had been standing, a silver zero printing itself into the 'T' of the 'TEXACO' pump he was hiding behind. Fuel bubbled and glugged onto the concrete beside Puccini's foot.

The Camry steadied, drove right at me, and I flattened against the back wheel of the police car, and took the gun from my waistband. The handgrip was slippery with sweat. Crouching, my knee to the concrete, my elbow below the stock to steady my arm against the yank of the recoil, I drew a breath that tasted of burnt rubber, and aimed.

A shot went off that wasn't mine. Over by the bathroom, David was on one knee, his cheek pressed to the stock of the sawn-off. He fired at the Camry. Its front tyre blew, shredded, sent up a cloud of white smoke, and the car went caroming through a couple of bins. David fired again. The windscreen burst. The Camry flipped. The guy with the gun slid headlong from the window, his arc as clean as an Olympic diver's, then went ploughing headlong across the forecourt on a thick, red-black smear of blood and bone and safety-glass. The car smashed through the window of the petrol-station shop, its wheels still turning. Brownish foam guttered up from a totalled soda machine. From inside the shop, there was the noise of glass sheeting across metal and the sound of a cardoor slamming. The cashiers screamed, yelled, ran.

Puccini shoved aside the bin he'd hidden behind, sprinted in a crouch across the forecourt, as a shadow appeared beyond the smashed window of the shop – tall, uniformed, armed, one leg dragging – and pushed open the convenience-store door. Gunfire sprayed the forecourt. Sparks flew. None caught. David ducked back into the bathroom.

Puccini opened the car-door. A shot twanged past, right between our heads. Even though the guy's leg was dragging, he'd tottered past the first set of pumps.

'Wait at the ramp,' said Puccini, and I ran so fast for the car that I heard a pop in the back of my knee that I knew would hurt when the adrenaline wore off. Getting into the car, I turned the key, floored it, the petrol-hose clunking against the side of the car, my hands so wet they squeaked on the wheel.

Puccini backed quickly across the forecourt, wild volleys of automatic fire making him duck his head. His hand closed around the empty coffee cup with one hand, then he grabbed the petrol-hose, lowered the nozzle to the cup, filled it, rolled it towards the shooter, and rolled himself across the concrete and fired twice, the first shot bursting the stock of the shooter's submachine gun, flinging spikes of plastic and metal into his neck and face, and, as he tugged, coughing, at the shards in his neck, Puccini's second bullet sparked against the stream of petrol. A scud of blue-orange fire licked across the concrete, up his thighs, his waist, his chest, and the gun fell from his hands.

Puccini stood, turned, and crossed to where I was waiting at the bottom of the ramp. David opened the bathroom door and came legging it across the concrete.

'You knew!' he shouted at Puccini. 'You knew they'd find us!'

Puccini shrugged.

'So we could draw some more of them out,' he said. 'And we could.' He got in the passenger side, shut the door, and said, 'And so – may we?'

Behind us, in the rear-view, the guy's bottom half was in flames. In the doorway of the convenience store, one cashier stood holding a fire extinguisher. The other two huddled behind her. She took one look at the guy on fire, dropped the extinguisher, and started to run, her two colleagues following.

'You're going to get us all killed,' David said.

'If you want me to do the job for them, I have no problem,' Puccini said.

David said nothing.

I took us onto the road and eased the pedal down as far as it would go. The needle climbed past a hundred and sixty. The whine of the tyres hurt my ears. A loose shard of grit hit the glass like a bullet and I jumped in my seat. The sweat running down me had that ammoniac tang of pure fear.

Puccini was toying with a carton of cigarettes he'd bought.

'Give me one of those,' I said.

'I don't think you want to do that.' Puccini raised his arms. His sleeves dripped petrol onto the knees of his combat pants.

My finger wagged in the air, and I started to say, 'Good point', but a jolt from behind cut me off. When I looked at the wing mirror it was just a nub of plastic that sizzled as it cooled.

'Shit,' David said, and ducked.

Puccini slid into the back of the car. He did something to the latch of the boot and it hissed open.

Cold air roared through the gap. In the rear-view mirror, another matt-black Camry was weaving back and forth across the dividing line, overtaking some cars, forcing others off the road, steadily closing in.

'And what's your fucking assumption about these ones?' David yelled. 'That we can handle these ones too?'

'You're not helping, man,' I said.

Puccini's pistol cracked once, twice, sparking between the tyres.

The air popped. In the rear-view mirror I saw a gloved hand holding a pistol-sized submachine gun. The next shot made a brake light tinkle and smash. David was sitting transfixed in his seat. The shotgun lay across his lap. He'd gone pale. When he met my eyes in the mirror he smacked the back of my headrest.

'Fuck you looking at?' he shouted. 'Eyes on the road.'

Puccini fired. The Camry's driver window went red. But then the back window of the Camry rolled down, and a bigger gun winked in the gap.

'Puta,' said Puccini, and shifted to the other side of the back seat and pulled down the boot of the jeep as a hailstorm-rattle of automatic fire shattered the back window, but I kept us steady, nicked us out of the way of one of those metallic-painted chicken-buses. The driver braked, but too sharply – the shot from the car behind us caught the side of the bus. Yells and screams cut the air. The bus's wheels skirled, then the driver stopped them at a diagonal across the two lanes, blocking the Camry's path, and I raised my head from where I'd dipped it, pressed the accelerator, heard cars whine by either side of us, the burst of speed leaving me loose-limbed, empty-headed, and I leaned into every curve and bend of the road until it felt like I was every curve and bend of the road, until all that was all there was in the whole world. Wind stung tears from my eyes. My every greedy breath tasted of hot tarmac and the sun-battered plants of the verge by the road.

'Want to swap?' Puccini said to David, watching him sponge his hands on his jeans.

David goggled at him.

'A joke.' He lowered his cheek to the stock of his pistol.

A second car rolled up a side-road ahead of us, out of a field of new furrows, a rifle leant against the sill of the back window. All my muscles seized.

'Eh,' I said.

Puccini looked over his shoulder, said, 'Go for him,' then lowered the back window, leaned out, and took a breath.

Their first shot put out a light. Their second dented the bonnet. Their third cracked the windscreen, scorched a hole in the passenger headrest, made me yell.

'Shh,' said Puccini, so close that his voice tickled my ear, that his breath dried the sweat on my neck.

The trigger clicked. The boom was so loud that I thought he'd burst my eardrum. The bonnet of the second Camry filled the windscreen, and I whipped the wheel around hard. As we sped past, I saw only the briefest flash of two bodies, one in the front, one in the back, red, smoking holes in their foreheads.

We cut out of a curve, into an empty space of road between two craggy walls of rock. Behind us, the first Camry had found a way past the bus. Ahead of us, in the lane opposite, was a red, eighteen-wheel truck. Puccini tried another pot-shot at the Camry, but missed, the echo of the ricochet twanging against the rocks, and I sneaked over the dividing line, sprinted the car forward, straight at the Coca-Cola truck.

Its shadow cooled the air inside the car. The Camry eased out of its lane, grew larger, gained. I took a deep breath. For a second it was just like home – me and two other idiots who lived nearby, in our dads' cars, mine a Corolla, theirs a van, on a strip of road lacquered with black mud, our engines revving, ready to speed at one another and see who braked or swerved first.

'Seatbelt,' I said.

My father was scarier than their father.

'What?' said Puccini.

That's why I always lost – diving into a hedge, braking so hard the tyres went bald, giving myself a whiplash injury so bad that I had to drop out of the school football team.

'Seatbelt,' I said, and lashed the car forward, my grip on the wheel so hard that I felt the burn split on the back of my hand, saw the bandage redden.

The bellow of the truck horn shook our windows. Puccini's fingers grabbed my headrest. So did David's.

The truck braked. The tyres screamed. A shot twanged past from behind us. A grey plume of burning rubber went up. This hiss of the truck-brakes and the blare of the horn made my head feel like it was about to split. The Camry behind us couldn't figure which way to swerve, tried one way, tried another, tried to turn, but then the back trailer swung and swiped them from view with a crash so rich that I shivered with the joy of it.

The cabin of the truck teetered and tottered and fell over on its passenger side. Our car rolled to a halt. For a moment there was no sound but the hiss of our cooling tyres.

'Did you see that?' I said. I could hear myself panting. A quick heat ran in my veins. I could feel every bit of my body, the lungs working, the muscles tight, the tendons humming with tension, every molecule shooting through a bright nothingness.

'See what?' said David.

The truck-cabin's door opened. The driver climbed out, stunned, pale, then hopped into the road and jogged around to where the back trailer had fallen over.

'I've ruined Christmas,' I said.

David sat back a little.

'You know.' I pointed. My finger was shaking. 'The ad. With the Santa driving the big truck. And I have just fucked up the truck. So Christmas is dead now.'

The truck-driver stopped when he got as far as the axle, his hands on his knees, and vomited at what he saw.

'Qué chingados,' David said.

Behind us, the smoke of the wrecked petrol station blackened the sky.

Puccini got out of the car, kneeled to the tarmac, and pulled what looked like a hubcap from the undercarriage. A red light blinked at its centre. He brought his heel down hard on the bulb then flung the thing towards the wreck. The truck-driver jumped at the clatter of it.

'Next side-road, please,' Puccini said. 'I think we've drawn enough of them on to us for now.'

'You're the boss.' I flipped the indicator, even though there was nobody, and turned the car back around.

25

The next time we stopped, the morning was clearing above fields of red barns and celandines and those little blue hallucinogenic manta de la Virgen squills. The engine off, I poured myself from the car to the warm tarmac like I was a shaken jelly, then crawled around the front, hauled myself up onto the bonnet, and just lay there, cruciform, the metal sun-warm and mosquito-flecked under my back as I stretched out. Carlos' ashes settled in their bag. In the field we'd stopped beside, a bull snorted in his sleep, beside a lake of floodwaters, while a mare went trotting through the long grass. The sky was so blue it looked wet. A dun flock of chachalacas burst chittering through the air above my head. The smog was a little lighter here: beyond the treeline of cedar and sorghum trees, I could see snow on the volcanoes, and the air had a fresh, alluvial nick to it, from where the road had been cut through a wall of limestone. The pale roots of an amate tree straggled through the rock, feeding off the water trapped in the strata.

Puccini was rooting in the boot, and David stood near the bonnet, looking at me with a smirk on his face.

'What, the driving tucker you out a little?'

'It wasn't the best.' I put my arms over my eyes.

'That was fucking crazy, man.' He shook his head. 'Where did you learn that?'

'There was very, very little to do where I was growing up.'

'Man, there wasn't anything to do where I was growing up, either, and I didn't turn out like that. Where'd he get you from?'

'Free in a cereal packet.'

David got up, laughing, and went a little way up the road, where an old couple stood grilling corn-cakes over a charcoal fire on the roadside. She had on traditional clothes, and he was wearing a cowboy hat, plaid shirt, and ancient Levi's. David struck up a conversation with them in a language I didn't recognise, all tongue-clicks and tapered inflections.

The car was shaking from whatever it was Puccini was doing at the back of it, so I got up and pissed onto a nest of syringes someone had dumped in the grass. Something splashed in the floodwaters that brimmed in the hedge, but I couldn't see what it was. Whatever it had been, though, it must have been big – the sound made me think of being at this Christmas party in Dublin at some Slovakian lad's house, and I'd gone to the jacks, heard something splashing around in the bath, and pulled back the shower curtain to find a sturgeon twitching its fins in its sleep.

'You're doing it wrong,' David yelled over to me, laughing. 'Don't aim uphill.'

'Fuck off,' I was about to say, but then I looked down, saw the piss roll in a puddle back down from the black roots of a pine by the gate. The toe-boxes of my Redwings were dark-ening in the stream. All I could say was, 'Fair enough.' There was a second splash, further up the hedge, but I was distracted by a horse that had wandered over, looking curious. By the gate, she snorted at me, bobbing her head.

'It's rude to compare,' I said, zipping up, then turned to see Puccini dragging a black body-bag out of the boot of the jeep, which he swung by the legs into the floodwater filling the ditch. When Puccini saw me, he nodded, clapping his hands together like they were dusty. The splash was as big as the other two I'd heard. A prickly shiver went over me. They must have been the bodies of the people we'd killed at the safehouse. The splash sent the horse scarper-ing off towards a copse of red-trunked palo mula trees at the far end of the field, but the old couple talking to David didn't seem to notice. Bubbles wobbled the surface of the water.

David wandered over from his side of the road, carrying three folded corn-leaves. Puccini said something to him in the language David had been speaking with the old couple. That was enough to get him beaming.

'You know this place pretty well, so,' David said, handing around the corn-cakes. 'Language and everything.'

Puccini nodded. 'We did a lot of work here in the '80s.'

'Wait,' I said. 'Weren't you in Salvador back then?'

Puccini gave me a pitying look and said, 'Half the time, we didn't know what country we were being sent to. You'd get into a helicopter, get out, there'd be a white man yelling at you, and that'd be it – kill the Indians, the Communists, the students, whoever, whether it was Salvador, Guatemala, Honduras, Nicaragua, wherever.'

Pictures from outside the Congreso came back to me, the photos Maya and I had seen, the photos showing families holding handkerchiefs made of torn bed-sheets.

'Here, though, we were chasing guerrillas that we'd driven out of Salvador,' he said. 'All of them had Greek names – Patroclus, Achilles, Ulysses, Ajax. We had an old German overseeing us.

'And I was very good at languages, so they gave me to him. He was very thorough. My job was to drive him around in an unmarked car while he graded the landscapes.'

'Graded for what?' David said.

'Different criteria for different purposes – ambushes, assassinations, large-scale murders. He'd recite numbers, characteristics, grades – "dark pool, five-hundred-year-old beech trees, no road – disposal: A1, secrecy: A2, isolation: A1, ease of exit: B2", all that. Zama, we called him. He looked like a ghost. Except for his eyelids – pink, like a rabbit's. He'd been with Röhm, gone to Bolivia in the late 1920s, worked for Trujillo later.' Puccini waved a hand at the horizon. 'We passed through here once – scouting a town taken by the guerrillas. Undercover, dressed as tourists. We said I was Italian. The town was nice – boys and girls kicking the same ball around, old people learning to write at schools in the park, that sort of thing. Children offered us sodas when we drove in. The only sign of anything military was a bell-tower where there were some women snipers in red berets, watching out, but even they were eating ice-creams. Zama said he could smell their wombs, wanted us to return, to shoot them, to dress the tree with their insides.'

David stared. He'd gone pale.

'But he'd already graded the zone an F2,' Puccini said, 'so it was easy to talk him out of it. All we did when we went back was to sneak into the church and put army uniforms on the saints, to scare people.'

'And Zama,' David said, his voice heavy. 'Where's he at now?'

'Murdered in France, I think.' Puccini started on the next half of his corn-cake.

'You think or you know?' David said.

'No comment.' Puccini wrapped up the lemon-hull and corn-crumbs, tossed the lot into the verge. A bubble popped in the black water of the ditch.

'How do you reckon he'd grade that field behind us?' I said.

'For a grave? B1,' said Puccini, then dusted off his hands and hopped up from the bumper. 'Horse might be an issue, though.'

The blister on the back of my hand was still seeping a red ooze, enough for Puccini to notice and click his tongue at the look of it.

'You should take a rest, I think,' he said. 'Let me drive.'

Puccini started the jeep again. The old couple selling the corn-cakes waved to us as we passed. Behind us, in the rearview, the floodwater filling the ditch was as still as glass.

26

No sirens or helicopters cut the air behind us. On the radio news, there was nothing about a blown-up petrol station. As the adrenaline wore off, my hand started to burn all over, and my tooth started to throb, while my banjaxed hamstring set up a saddened twanging at the back of my knee. After an hour or so, Puccini slowed the jeep through a long straggling town at the confluence of three large highways.

'This is my old neck of the woods,' David said from the back seat.

Headlights flickered on streams of red mud. Our windscreen blurred. It was like driving through a tunnel. The air was thick with diesel fumes and the honk of buses, and what passed for a pavement was a busy cram of men in fieldworkers' clothes and women wearing faux-fur-collared puffa jackets over long patterned skirts.

'Vibrant,' I said.

'Hey, fuck you, man.'

'I mean it. I love places like this.'

David narrowed his eyes.

'What? They're cute.'

'You're weird, man,' he said. 'Real weird. I got out of here as soon as I could.'

'Come on, man,' I said. 'None of us wants to be here, and we still have to go to fucking Walmart.'

'You were undercover, no?' Puccini said to David.

'Yeah,' he said. 'How'd you know?'

'The way you act,' Puccini said.

A berg of dead leaves slid along the kerb, the same yellow-orange as the flowers at Carlos' funeral. Scuds of primary-school-age kids fled yapping and giggling among them, pelting back from school through the rain.

'Undercover, then,' I said.

'Yeah,' he said.

'What age?'

'Nineteen,' he said. 'They put me in a Mara.' He drew up the sleeve of his shirt, where I could see a Superman 'S' wrapped around an 'M' and a '13'. 'They did it with a guitar-string and a car-battery and a bit of a ball-point. It didn't hurt, because it's a shitty tattoo.'

Puccini eased the jeep through the blare of horns and the whine of scooters, through a roundabout of muck-specked hydrangeas ringing a bust of Arbenz.

The road eased upwards through firs and pines, growing foggier and colder with each bend until the space beyond the trees was grey and opaque, past houses whose flat roofs were coated in neon-green moss, past a shimmer of lake-water and flame trees in the gaps between the treeline, and on through a sad dark town where the birds seemed to have learned to imitate the beep lorries make when they're backing up.

'Undercover is hard,' Puccini said.

'It is.' David rolled his sleeve down. 'Like being an actor.'

An older woman stood talking to her son under the shelter of the bandstand. He lay in a long wooden cart, his arms bent, his feet turned inwards, gesturing at the grape-red clouds with his wrist while she nodded.

'No stunt-double, though,' said Puccini.

'No director saying "Cut", either.'

On the square, under an umbrella, a man of fifty in a cheap suit was having his shoes shined, one foot up on a wooden box, munching a sandwich, his gaze aimed at a girl in a school uniform who jogged across the road.

After that we snaked out along the dirt roads and on through a marshy nowhere where the tree-trunks looked like bones and their branches looked like black veins against the white air and the grey mud. It was properly bucketing by now, and the drum of rain had my head hopping. There was only one house that I could see, an odd three-storey thing with the railings eaten hollow by rust, the roof sharp, the faux-Tudor panelling gone brown in the wet air, and the shadow of its bulk falling over piles of rusting ship and car and tractor parts, poked through by tall stands of nettles and scutch-grass. The roof was piled with discarded mufflers of all shapes and sizes.

The garage of the house rattled open at our approach. A husky-looking guy in an oil-stained vest under a padded denim jacket stood in the gap, plucking at a beard that looked like a worn-out Brillo pad with one hand. He held the tape-wrapped handle of a knife in the other.

Puccini sat up, lowered his window, and held up a hand. The bearded guy opened the door the rest of the way. The knife dropped slowly to his side.

'Old colleague,' Puccini said.

He rolled the jeep into the garage's clean smell of paint and rubber. Chains and hooks hung from nails on the wall. In the corner sat a large toolbox with its lid half-off and belt after belt of long gold bullets layered one on top of the other inside.

'Was he expecting us?' I said.

Puccini shook his head.

'Just me.'

The mechanic stood to one side of the garage, guarding a wooden door, gave me the dead-fish eye as I got out of the car.

'He a cop?' he said. His accent was Salvadorean, his voice hoarse, his shoulders bunched like he was used to leaning into punishment.

'Uh, press, actually,' I said.

'Same thing,' said the mechanic. He cleared his throat, chin-jutted at David. 'And this one?'

'Afraid so,' he said. 'But just homicide.'

The mechanic coughed out a laugh.

'What's homicide?' he said. He didn't put the knife down. Up close, I could see that it was a hacksaw blade mounted on a triggered handle, the guard made of beaten metal. He was studying my face.

'He's harmless, Sarabia,' said Puccini.

Sarabia shook his head. 'It's not that.' He laid the knife down on a cardboard box, chuckling a little. 'Man, Evelio, he looks like Morsa, doesn't he?'

Puccini laughed, leaned his hand on the bonnet of the police car.

'Twins,' said the mechanic. 'I swear.' He laid down the knife to trace the shape of a moustache above his lip with two fingers. 'It's this thing. Like a walrus' tusks. So, you know – Morsa, we called him.' He clapped me on the shoulder. 'You go upstairs. Look like you're dying, Morsita, holy shit.'

'Who's Morsa?' David said.

'We'll tell you later, cop.' Sarabia clapped him on the shoulder. 'Go on, go upstairs. We got work for you.'

David opened the door and I followed him. The carpet was tracked all over with black boot-prints, but the walls were knotty pine, hung with old framed photos of army football teams, clippings from the sports pages, iron farm implements. The fridge's motor rucketed like it had about a week left before conking out. Out back a huge, sinewy banyan shaded the yard, the grass yellowed around its trunk.

The adrenaline was all gone now. A bastard of a headache was booting me behind the eyes. A Rorschach blot of greasy sweat showed on the front of my shirt. The odour of the men who'd attacked me tacked to my body, sweat and brands of hair-gel and deodorant that I'd never wear, greasy on my fingers and neck and hands. After taking two cups from the draining-board, I filled them from the sink and handed one to David.

'Man, I was so sick of this shit, way before I left under-cover,' he said. 'Just random shit. You go out in the morning, you don't know what the fuck is going to happen that day, where you'll sleep, anything like that. *If* you'll sleep that day, even.' He gulped the water. 'Christ, my wife, she was so jit-tery from it all, she got on her knees and thanked God – right there in the kitchen – when I told her I'd gotten my promo-tion to homicide.'

'Which is hardly a walk in the park, either.'

'Not even a little.'

There were still a few donuts in my seabag from the plane before, so I made coffee from some of the instant I found in the press, took our cups over to the table, slid the box over to David. Rain and seeds fell pattering through the banyan's leaves and branches, while rats skittered through the underbrush.

'Might as well embrace the cop cliché,' I said, 'if that's all they're going to call us.'

He laughed.

'Hey, at least they gave you a nickname.'

I looked at the coffee-soaked hoop of dough, wanted the action to feel different somehow, now that there were people dead because of me, but all that happened was my mouth filled with spit, my throat ached to swallow, same as ever, because *normal* can mean anything you want it to, and all you need to feel hungry is to be safe.

The door clicked open. Puccini stepped through, carrying his two sports-bags. The din of whirring and spraying behind him grew louder. In the second before he shut the door, I saw a huge black SUV standing on the ramp where the jeep we'd stolen had been. Sarabia's feet protruded from under the rear bumper. Blue-white light rippled the undercarriage, and there came the high static noise of acetylene cutting metal.

David gave a low whistle.

'That a monster truck?' he said.

'In a manner of speaking,' Puccini said, and closed the door behind him.

'Want one?' I said, reaching into the seabag for another donut box.

Puccini wagged a finger, then dropped the sports-bags on the table.

'You can eat and work, right?' he said. His sleeves were rolled up to the elbow, and I could see that his forearms were scored red from the car's broken safety glass.

'More or less,' said David.

'This is easy.' Puccini unzipped the bag. I could see lengths of steel piping, bags of cotton-wool, and a tangle of fuses.

'Oh, I know how to do this.' David took out one of the steel pipes, and began to tamp cotton-wool down it. 'Silencers, right?' He forced a gap in the cotton-wool with a screwdriver, then clipped the fuses so that they clamped the wadding tight to the wall of the pipe. He rummaged in the sports-bag then, took out a can of oil, and pressed the spout to the centre of the wadding before turning the bottle upside-down.

'And you,' Puccini said, unzipping a compartment of the sports-bag, 'sharpen these.'

He handed me a whetstone and a handful of tent-pegs.

'For?'

'To climb a brick wall,' he said.

The cold metal weight of the tent-pegs felt a lot like the sensation in my stomach, hearing that, and I remembered the floor-plan of the governor's house, the one Puccini had been so eager to get his hands on.

'Well, get to work,' Puccini said, leaving the room again. 'We have to go shopping.'

27

Sharpening the tent-pegs took longer than David took with the silencers, so he helped me out. We were just finishing up when the door opened and Sarabia came in, carrying a plastic bag that held a stack of polystyrene trays.

'Dig in, Morsita.' His pores breathed that metal-blue hum that my father used to get after a day in his workshop.

The dark soup I ate was tasty, but hard to finish, because the chickpeas floating in it made me see teeth floating in a slurry of blood.

Sarabia pointed at a chunk of fried cheese in my tray.

'You going to eat that, Morsita?' he said.

'Eventually,' I said.

'You're going to have to tell us who this Morsa guy was, man.' David lifted the lid of his tray.

'Just a journalist,' said Sarabia, hunkering over his food. 'Long hair, long moustache, big glasses. Same as you.'

'Same as us, too, really,' said Puccini, loading his fork. 'When we were in disguises.'

'The idea was to look like the enemy,' said Sarabia. 'Like hippies. Wear balaclavas all day, sneak out at night. We had these Russian weapons taken from the rebels, so whatever we did it would look like they had done it.'

David had gone pale again.

'You did a lot of damage to our people,' he said quietly.

'Who did you lose?' Puccini said.

'Me, personally? Nobody. But my father did. My mother. My uncles. Their schoolfriends.'

Sarabia lifted his head from his food.

'But that wasn't you, was it?' he said.

'Well, I wasn't born, so – no.'

'Then it wasn't your problem.' Sarabia hunkered back to his plate.

'It's not my problem, but it's my history,' David said.

Sarabia coughed out another laugh.

'History's the story of people caring about shit that either doesn't matter or doesn't work,' he said. 'And everybody dies at the end of that story.'

David shook his head, but went back to eating.

'In the mornings,' said Puccini, continuing like nothing had happened, 'we'd collect the journalists, take them to the site of the massacre, invite them to join us as we liberated the town from the Communists.'

'Morsa, he was with some big US outlet.' Sarabia removed a plastic lid from one of the beakers of mango juice that he'd bought. 'And so we met him here – near Nebaj. Must have been '86.' He shook drops of condensation from the bag of tortillas and tore one in half. 'Morsa didn't like what he saw.'

He forked up a lump of fried cheese. He snorted. 'Poor Morsa.'

David looked at him, his hand gripping his glass.

Puccini swirled his canteen and smiled and said, 'The only reason I remember Morsa is because he got up in our faces, challenging us to *"bring peace to this tragic nation"*.'

'Which we were doing, frankly,' Sarabia said. 'By some definitions.'

Puccini crossed to the sink and refilled his canteen.

'His voice was wobbling when he talked,' said Sarabia. 'You remember that? Didn't like the flies. Didn't like the body smell. Didn't know we'd put them there. Plucking his moustache like this.' Sarabia imitated him, laughing, then said, 'Do you get like that, Morsita?'

A hot flare of anger and self-disgust cut through me, but all I did was swirl my água de mango, and say, 'Not any more, sadly.'

Puccini reached for Sarabia's empty tray and loaded the remains of his food into it.

'You sure?' Sarabia wiped his mouth.

Puccini nodded.

'We have a trip to make,' he said. 'Walmart.'

'When it's this dark?' Sarabia frowned. 'There's a lot of movement around, last few days.'

'We'll be OK.' Puccini brought the empties and the cutlery over to the sink, then turned to David and I. 'Five minutes,' he said. 'Be ready.'

'Take one of the shitty cars,' Sarabia said. 'Don't be getting noticed.'

'OK.' Puccini slipped through the door and into the garage.

'Fucking Evelio, man.' Sarabia shook his head, speared a chunk of stewed beef. 'You're lucky he likes you two. Otherwise you'd be dead.' His laugh sounded clotted. He ran a finger down the middle of his face, from forehead to chin. 'He tell you about this?'

'Some punishment deal,' I said, and drained my glass. 'Yeah.'

'Rap he took for me.' He pressed a tortilla into the remaining bean-juice. 'We were, what, twelve? And he could take the heat, but I couldn't. Me, I was from a nice family. All that early start shit, all that no meals shit, I couldn't take it. First few months, I was a pussy. Dropped the ball. Let a prisoner go. I mean, someone else caught her, did what he had to, whatever, so it's not like I made a difference. But Evelio, he said it was him let her go.' He stripped fat from a chunk of meat. 'He was like my older brother.'

I sawed my cheese in half, held up one section on the end of the knife.

'Nah,' Sarabia said. 'I'm good now.'

'Alright. Well, thanks, or whatever.'

My tray was empty, so I got up from the table. David followed me. As I opened the door, Sarabia gave me a salute, and said, 'Well, keep fighting the good fight, Morsita.'

28

We pulled up outside Walmart in the battered red Chevy that Puccini had taken from Sarabia's garage. The automatic doors pinged open as the three of us passed through, and the pristine nick of mints and carpet shampoo in my nose cut open a space in my head that led all the way back to Saturday mornings trailing my mother around the supermarket. Inside, the warm light and the piped radio hits, the evening shoppers nudging trolleys from aisle to aisle, all that dulled normality, after everything that had happened, made me want to cry.

At the electronics section, Puccini stuck a Post-It with the product serial number on it for the kid behind the counter to pick up, then sent David and I over to hardware and homewares with a list – styrofoam pool-noodles, fuel oil in five-gallon tins and three huge bags of fertiliser, oil and nails, jerrycans of bleach and drain-cleaner.

'Hey, that fertiliser.' David leaned over the trolley, peering at the back of the bag. 'Does it have that chemical in it? The kind he told us to get. What's it called?'

'Ammonium nitrate,' I said. 'And yes, it does.'

'Very normal selection of stuff,' David said, as he dropped the biggest tube of Superglue I've ever seen into the trolley.

'What's that for?'

'Cuts,' he said. 'In an emergency. You put some on the edges of a cut, press 'em shut.' He showed me his forearm. There was a white trace like a load of 'Z's stuck together, end to end. 'Knife fight.'

'Jesus.'

'Don't see us having a problem paying for all this, not at all,' David said. 'Did you see what he was getting over at electronics? Like, eight drones, or something?'

'I'm sure I've been put on a watchlist for less,' I said.

We went back to find Puccini, but he was already turning around. Three DVD burners, a bunch of Zippo lighters, and twelve-packs of Coke and beer in glass bottles loaded his trolley.

'What, we that thirsty?' David said, flicking the cardboard skirting of the beers.

A chain of pops like firecrackers cut through the Britney Spears song playing from the speakers. A box of granola exploded behind my head in a puff of sizzled oats and gunsmoke. Nothing of me could move, no matter how hard my brain screamed at me to run. David and Puccini dropped, pulling me to the ground with them, and my head knocked against the wheel of a woman's trolley. She looked at us like we were nuts, but then a bullet cut a smoking hole in the lino. She looked at us, then at the hole, and backed away from her trolley, faster and faster, until she was full-on sprinting past the tills.

The security guard went running from the doors, but he had barely a chance to turn around before a shot got him, and he stumbled forward, frowned at the blood on his hand, then fell over, with a bloody tunnel through his cheek. A second security guard jogged from the side of the shop nearest the ATMs, but a shot snapped his head back, a rope of blood broke thickly through the air, his knees turned inwards, and he toppled over by the tills.

Some of the lights went out. The screaming started. There was the jangle of knocked-over trolleys, the rustle of dropped bags. Someone yelled. There was a wettish thud of impact. A man sobbed. A woman shrieked and ran and fell. I watched Puccini slide across the aisle on his belly, then sigh as he got to his feet and pressed his back against a wall of Frosties. David and I were still on the floor. The air tasted of dust and berry-scented floor-cleaner. Then the rest of the lights went off

'I'll be back,' David hissed, and slunk off.

I still couldn't move. My body was pins and needles all over. All I could see now were flickering pink dots ticking back and forth. There was a hiss and a choking smell and the smoke alarms began to wail, cutting off the Britney best-of. From where I lay, I heard feet stampede past me, heard pistols cracking, felt someone step on my hand, heard a load of fruit go tumbling from the display pyramids, and the thud of running feet become a squelching. Where to crawl, how fast to crawl, whether to roll, whether to run, every one of those questions, they slammed down inside my head, leaving my mind frantic and pinned between them like walls. The noises of the fight split into things they reminded me of – a riot out the back of the Estadio Azteca, the night I'd been to see Cruz Azul play América, blooming white clouds of tear-gas, the clank and clatter of hooves and coshes – but then a flash of light appeared above me, the muzzle of a P90 swung up, and my ears braced for the chatter that would kill me, except then came a thud, and the man's head disappeared in a white cloud. For a second he gaped at me, his face coated and gurning under the detergent tipping over his head, and a second, deeper boom burst his face over me. As he fell, the flashlight of his gun lit up the person who'd shot him – David, smiling, the sawn-off shotgun in his hand, opening his mouth to say something, but a gun went off, and he coughed like he'd been winded, and stooped over, his gun clattering to the lino, looking like he was drowning in the air, his arms and legs hanging, flailing, suddenly heavy to him, his eyes big, and stupid, and scared, and he fell over, whimpering, clutching his stomach, his legs drawn up like those of a soaked roach.

Now I tried to get up, but something dumped me to my knees, so hard that the noise hurt my ears. Pictures blitzed through my head – a jet contrail cutting white across sheer blue, a green hood of alcatraz leaves low over me, a space of blue smoke, my roar of fear lost in the roar of a washing-machine, my fingers whitening then reddening under the slam of a door on my fingers, my eyes shut, my hands over my ears, my mother shouting, my mind flipping and re-flipping pictures from my grandfather's encyclopaedias, pictures that showed safe green places to hide, that showed high blue Kodachrome nowhere. And then the pain hit, so hard and sudden I thought the boss of my skull was about to split, and light blazed behind my eyelids, and all the pictures vanished, left me in a mell of gunshots and running feet, loud one second, dying away the next as I was jerked from my knees. My head whooshed like I'd been dunked face-first into water. When I tried to breathe, the air was gone, and I heard a *thup* that meant my head was in a plastic bag again.

Another gun went off. Somebody fell over. Thumbnails cut through the bag, right over my eyes. Air burned my lungs. A hand was on my back. A voice I knew from somewhere said, 'I'm sorry, Andrew. We needed to draw more of them on.' Then I was too tired to know what was happening, or even who it was happening to.

The last thing I saw was light dripping from palm-fronds that hooded a swimming pool. That picture was from years ago, some weekend getaway with Helen at her parents' house in Yautepec, soon after I'd moved over. If I'd had longer with that picture maybe I'd have wondered if that was the last time I had ever been happy, and that's why my brain threw it up, or if it was just because the burn of the air in my lungs had made me think of swimming, in some buried, reptile sector of my brain. But I didn't have too long with the picture, and what I thought next wasn't quite in words, so much as a sleepy noticing that the action of my thoughts, the whole of my life as I'd known it, both those things were a lot like that light on the water – a pretty coincidence, a bright nothing, a fractal accident, soon gone.

Carlos and I were back in Poza Rica, a wind chasing perfect spirals of soot around our ankles – zeroes, eights, infinity
signs. He was swatting mosquitoes away from the Y-incision
whose leakage was darkening his white shirt. Julián Gallardo,
the dead kid we'd found that time, he was there, too, lying
on the bar in his coffin. Carlos drew a blanket of purple and
orange cempasúchil flowers over the body, their green stems
woven together in a lattice. An AM radio was playing bolero
songs – 'So hard of heart,' sang the lovelorn tenor voices.

'It was meant to be just another story,' I told him. My
voice was sloppy, my hand gestures baggy.

'There's no such thing, vato,' Carlos said.

'Nobody asked us to look,' I said. My voice was a whine.
My head was resting on my forearms. 'It's not fair.'

'Drunken madness,' sang the AM radio.

'Yeah, man, I know,' Carlos said. He gave Julián Gallardo's
bloodied hair a pat. The five-peso candles leaked clear wax
into the shot-glasses laid in a ring around the kid's head and
shoulders, their light camera-flash-white over the statues at

his feet – Santa Barbara ringed with flickering black candles, Saint Jude with his quiff of fire, a Santa Muerte in a blue feather boa, Maximón in jungle camo.

Carlos gave the kid a creased-mouth smile and got to his feet, then said, 'Now nothing can ever look the same again.'

He stood back from the body, his hands crossed over his belt-buckle. He was wearing his white Elvis Presley suit and those penny loafers that looked like pistol-silencers with buckles on them.

'Don't cry on my shrine, vato,' Carlos said, laughing gently. 'You'll wreck my work.'

'It's gorgeous,' I said, and lit a cigarette to put in Julián's mouth. He had no lips – the police had taken them with the rest of his face – so I opened and shut his jaws, clamping his teeth around the butt. After that I fixed his shirt-collar so the bruises around his neck didn't show, then went to stand next to Carlos. Ash kept blowing out of his sleeves, greying the suit I'd worn to his funeral, but that didn't matter, it was just nice to be around him again. His fingers patted my shoulder.

'I'm really sorry, man,' I said.

'Relax,' said Carlos. 'We're having fun, aren't we?'

Ants crawled over the sectioned papaya and watermelon we'd laid at his feet, beside bird-of-paradise flowers and black orchids in clear glass vases. We put down candles, two tones of red: dark for pericardial fluid, light for the bruises around Carlos' neck, then took deep drags on our cigarettes, breathing them over Julián's body like incense, but it was all of those other gone people that I was thinking of.

'A cleaning can be a beautiful thing,' Carlos said.

'I don't know.' I turned a coffee cup on its saucer. 'Might wake up soon. I'm not sure how much longer I can take it here.'

Carlos laughed. His smile was as heatless a crescent as the sliver of moon shining through the charred rafters, through the holed roof.

'You aren't gonna like it much out there, neither, vato.'

'Wait, though,' I said, and grabbed his arm. 'Is she there, too?'

'Is who there, vato?'

Snow and crumpled MISSING posters were blowing around our ankles, one for Julián Gallardo, one for his father, one for each of the dead and disappeared in all the stories I'd written as a reporter in Mexico, and one for Helen, too, the photo from her student card, the photo she hated, showing her glowering at the camera, her blonde bob pristine, perfect, her Michel Foucault polo-neck up to her chin.

'This one,' I said, grabbing Helen's picture, shoving it in his face. 'Helen. Have you seen her there?'

Carlos made a crease of his mouth and shook his head.

'Sorry, vato,' he said, but he was crumbling to ash. 'I'm nowhere, and so is she. So it's hard to check.'

'Oh, stick around, won't you?' I said, but then a wind blew him away, a hot wind that felt red on my skin, and felt like a scream in my ears, and then I was awake, the light sizzling, a smell of sweat and piss and blood loud in my nose.

The room was windowless, walled with ceramic tiles, ceilinged in bare brick, and David was sitting on a kitchen chair opposite me, gagged with a bloody sock, his wrists and feet bound with razor-wire. The space under his nails brimmed dark red, drops running down his hands from where they'd flayed the skin out with a needle. Blood had seeped out around the sock, the run-off turning the hairs on his chest to wet black whorls. A leech-shape coated in dust on the floor. His breath was fast and shallow, his eyes unfocused, and now and then he'd scream against the sock, a blaring like a hurt bull.

Someone was moving my hand for me. When I looked, my right hand was draped half in, half out of a drawer.

'This one's awake, chief,' said a voice.

A boot rested against the edge of the drawer. The guy wearing the boot was the Guatemalan cop from the tunnel, the one with the thinning, slicked-back hair.

He winked at me, kicked the drawer shut, and the noise was gravel crunching. The cop grabbed me by the hair and flung me to the ground. The wind went out of me, it was like my chest was a pricked balloon, and grit scraped my ear. The cop was still pulling my head up. There was a dull thwack and a sudden heat and I saw him swing back the knife Sarabia had been holding at the garage door. Blood ran down the side of my face. My head rang like a gong. My ear was in two halves, and both of them hurt.

Mangueras stepped out from behind my chair and looked down at me and said, 'We just want to know where he went. That shouldn't be a problem. He showed you no loyalty. So. Where did he go?'

'I didn't see.' The pain was a red yell in my head that I had to shout over. My hand looked like a stepped-on bag of peanuts. Vomit climbed my throat.

Mangueras sighed, shook his head, pinched the bridge of his nose, then flicked a hand at the cop.

The cop walked towards David, took a Zippo from his pocket and grabbed David by the hair. The panic in David's eyes, I swear, it made every hair of my body shrill, like someone was sawing a violin-bow over the ends of my nerves, and that made me hate him, made me want him dead already, so I wouldn't have to look.

'Let me help you out here.' Mangueras sounded tired. He turned a chair around backwards to sit on it. He put a fist at the small of his back, arched forward and gave a little grunt of satisfaction, his paunch nudging the chair, then loosened his tie. 'His daughter, right?'

The cop took the gag out of David's mouth and drew the Zippo-flame towards one eye. The lashes sizzled. The smell was like burning Lycra. David's pleas weren't words any more, but they were very fucking loud.

'That's probably a good guess, right?' Mangueras' voice was gentle. 'You want to tell me where that is?'

David was nothing but noise and pain now, like a gut-shot fox.

'C'mon, you know you want to help,' said Mangueras, his voice gentle, inveigling, almost soothing. 'You're a nice guy.'

I watched the urine pool around David's ankles. He had no eyelashes left on one eye, and the lid was black, starting to blister. He'd wailed himself past tiredness. His sobs were just a way to breathe. The fear in him now was older than he was, older than the world.

'He knows nothing, man.' I couldn't keep my voice level. The whine in it made me hate myself. My tongue felt fat and dry. 'He needs a hospital, man, c'mon.'

Mangueras put a hand to his forehead, made a frustrated noise, and said, 'OK.'

The cop lifted David's eyelid, pressed the Zippo-flame to the white. The pop was a foot stepping on bubble-wrap. David howled.

'Shit,' said the cop, shaking blobs of goop from his fingers.

'He went after the governor,' I said. 'He doesn't want to go near his daughter. He wants to keep her safe. Please.'

'Hah,' said the cop, and lifted David's head. His eye was a red-rimmed crater. He'd either passed out or died of shock.

'He didn't go after the governor,' said Mangueras, 'because we have the governor.'

The cop went to the corner, plugged something in, stepped back into view holding an electric drill.

'The US has a nice offer,' said Mangueras. 'So do the Mexicans.'

Now it was dawn in the bar where Carlos and I had been all these nights. Helicopters thrummed against the pink air. Time was no longer a flow of events so much as a big shaking in a black nowhere, like when I was a toddler and my mother would shut me in the back kitchen with the washing machine on. She'd leave the door unlocked sometimes – the drink would have her half-gone half the time – but that made no difference. She was never so wasted that she couldn't hit your throat with an apple from across the kitchen.

A plane cut across the blue inside my head. Carlos was on the stage of the bar, singing Elvis Presley's 'If I Can Dream' in front of a shaking red curtain. The roof had been blown off, most of the walls had collapsed, and thin black trees reached above the rafters, resolving back into smoke as I looked at them.

'Wake him up,' said the cop. 'I'm busy here.'

'Hey, who's the boss?' said Mangueras, but he jammed his thumbs into my temples. The dream broke. The cop had the drill going in the soft join of David's right shoulder. He had no screams left in him, just moans like someone stuck in a bad dream. My shiver, watching, was like someone rinsing out my backbone with a powerhose.

My eyes shut. Snow and ash drifted down over Carlos and me alone in the bar.

Mangueras slapped my face. The cop pressed the drill into David's stomach wound, and he made sounds I'd heard only in films – crunchy gurgles, watery pleas.

The cop finished up. David lay prone in the chair. The cop knelt over me, so close that I could smell the breath from his nose.

Love, if you get this, it's like I told you – death has a dozen smells, and David's was the stuff on that drill.

'The US wants the governor, but to nail him, they need a witness,' said Mangueras, 'and they want Puccini.'

The drill-bit nudged between the buttons of my shirt and I kicked, bucked, thrashed, like a fish on a riverbank.

Mangueras lit a cigarette with the spattered Zippo.

The cop held down the trigger of the drill. The fabric of my shirt twisted, tore, smoked.

'You can make it stop if you just tell us where he is.'

My navel hair twined around the drill bit, pulled free, left a bleeding stipple of holes. The noise of my own scream hurt my ears.

'The Walmart!' I wailed. The pain made the vowels came out all baggy and shapeless.

'We checked. He's not there. And so' – Mangueras pressed a thumb and forefinger to the bags under his eyes – 'the address, please. Or even just the neighbourhood. A description. Anything.'

A radio on the cop's belt blurted static. He let go the trigger of the drill, pressed a finger to the worm of plastic coiling into his ear.

'Whoa,' he said.

'Whoa what?' Mangueras tensed in the chair.

The cop held up a finger, listened for a moment. Mangueras' cigarette hung halfway to his mouth.

'Never mind.' The cop pressed the drill harder against my belly. 'It was "Whoa, nothing".'

'What?' snapped Mangueras.

The cop sighed, lifted the drill away from me, and glared at Mangueras.

'The guy just stopped talking,' he said. 'OK? "Whoa, nothing".'

Mangueras' eyes widened.

'Wait,' he said, and drew his gun, tried to get to his feet, but the doorway to the basement blew out, knocked him to the ground in a cloud of coal-dust, brick-chunks, instantly charred laths of wood. Sharded ribs tumbled across the floor.

The cop had been flung onto his ass in the dirt. He shuffled through the filth, both hands up, saying, 'Hey, now, you wait.'

A shot burst his eye, and he fell back, the hole gushing red.

On the ground, Mangueras was trying to get his gun up, but Puccini was already across the floor, stepping out of the dust-cloud. He grabbed Mangueras' arm, snapped the wrist over his knee, then knocked him out with an elbow to the back of the head. He walked over to me, lifted the plastic tie holding my wrists together, pinched the latch between his fingers until it snapped.

'I'm very sorry, Andrew,' he said.

'Tell it to him.' I gave a backward nod at David.

Puccini looked over like he was seeing David for the first time, then strode across to him, put two fingers to his neck, clicked his tongue.

'Has he got long?' I got to my feet, massaging my wrists.

'Not really, no.' Puccini took out a multi-tool, snipped at the razor-wire, then eased David out of the chair and carried him in a fireman's lift towards the remains of the stairwell. After collecting the Zippo – a little dinged from the fall – I followed on behind him, stepping over a body that lay on the stairs, his face bewildered. As we reached the carpet upstairs, Mangueras started to stir and groan downstairs, so I pulled shut the top basement door, heard the lock click.

'You get his gun?' I said.

Puccini held up the pistol.

'We don't want him killing himself,' he said.

Upstairs was a ruin. Puccini had crashed the Chevy through the front of the house. The bonnet was lodged in the stairs. Two drones were crumpled smoking on the floor. Sharded beer- and Coke-bottles carpeted the corridor. Most of the front wall was rubble. The body of the man lying there had smoking gouges all down his back, yellow adipose marbling his bared interior.

'Fertiliser and fuel oil,' said Puccini. 'Like your country-men in the North.'

'Kind of,' I said, a hand to my mouth. The wind was lifting a tallowy smell over us. Years of drinking mean that I'm pretty good at wedging down the urge to puke, but that was almost the limit. 'Where's Sarabia?'

Puccini jerked his head. His lips were pursed so hard that a white ring appeared around them. I turned around and saw a large tank in the middle of the kitchen, right in front of the doorway, covered by a black cloth that was holed with burns and singed at the edges from a styrofoam pool-noodle stuck flaming to the lino.

'What did they do to him?' I managed to say.

'The same things I am going to do to Mangueras,' Puccini said, then walked towards the front door.

'How many were there?' I said, following him. Outside, two jeeps were in flames. The melted shape of another drone was visible between them.

'About eight,' Puccini said. 'But it's easy when they're scared.' He walked across what was left of the porch and laid David on a reclining chair. Night was fading towards morning. Winds pushed clouds over the hills.

'There's a first-aid kit in the car,' said Puccini.

'I think he needs a bit more than that.'

'There is morphine in the kit. Now, if you wouldn't mind.' He was tearing his own shirt into strips, tying them around the red flitters left of David's wrists, then wadding cloth against the hole in his gut.

'Right,' I said, and went back inside. My ear was still streaming, and halved at the root, so I went to the kitchen, tied a tea towel to the side of my head, and continued towards the door. Mangueras was charging his shoulder against the top door, so I kicked it to frighten him quiet, before picking my way over the wrecked steps. One snapped under me and my leg stabbed through into the space beneath. Grabbing onto the car's door-handle gave me a second to stick my foot between two banister rails and climb up onto the bonnet. From there, I was able to open the door and climb in and find the first-aid kit lying under the passenger seat.

'Careful,' said Puccini, when I got back to the terrace. David's arm was limp. His chest was barely moving. Puccini had to keep swatting mosquitoes from the hole over his eye.

'With what?' I handed him the case.

'The car door,' he said. 'Don't slam it.'

Puccini filled a syringe from a clear bottle. He had to spend a while tapping up a vein on David's arm, the pulse was that weak. Puccini crossed David's hands over his chest, then pulled a blanket over him. He got up, saw my hand, and said, 'Can you make a fist?'

'Haven't tried.' I tried. 'Oh. Jesus.'

'Broken,' said Puccini. He filled another syringe. 'The knuckles.'

He lifted off the top layer of the first-aid kit, scissored the makings of a sling from some gauze, wrapped my hand so tight that my fingertips tingled and stuck a safety-pin through the sling over my shoulder. He tapped the syringe.

'Wait, I don't like them,' I said. 'Needles.'

'Do you like pain?'

'Not massively,' I was about to say, and then there was the bee-sting of the needle going into the bruised skin between my knuckles, followed by a flood of numbness.

'Here.' Puccini took a handful of cigarettes from his packet of Balis. 'Sit with him. He won't take long. And I'll be down there for a while.' He got up and went back inside. I heard the basement door open and shut and tried not to shiver. Some Disney prince I didn't recognise grinned up at me from the blanket. I couldn't look at the whites of his eyes.

Bone-colour trees I couldn't name pocked the yellowish marshland stretching away all around us. No birds sang. Rain misted down. David's chest rose and fell jerkily under my hand. Times like that, you want to put them out of their misery, you honestly do, but if that's all they've got left, it doesn't seem fair.

Low pressure pulled veils of cloud down over the hills. David's breath rasped, weakened. The swirl of clouds wove, knitted, turned opaque. The hills could have been a coastal promontory swallowed by fog, and that sent my mind all sorts of places – me and Carlos on that Veracruz highway siding on the last day I'd seen him alive, the loft room in Uruguay, me and Helen and Callum in my ma's Ford Focus, heading to Callum's parents' beach home in Wexford, gulls flinging past on the salt wind.

The rain came down in a big hush over the waste ground, grass traced the path of the wind, and the bark of the guanacaste trees turned to jungle-camo patterns in the rising light.

David's wallet was poking out of his pocket. Inside was a police-issue credit card with his photo on it. Sticking out between the receipts and bills I found a photo, seamed from the folding and unfolding of the wallet, and I took it out, saw David with his arm around a woman his age, him in jeans and a black shirt, her in a Ramones spaghetti-strap top and a traditional skirt, holding their ringed fingers up to the camera, cloudy hills and a neon pink sunset behind them. For a while I just sat there looking at them, one hand holding the photo, the other hand on the bulge of Carlos' ashes inside the jacket I had on.

The hills were invisible now. Puffs of fog as thick as cotton-wool hovered over the grass. All I could hear was the rain, my breath, the creak of moss-coated oaks beyond the wall. The next time I remembered to check David's breathing, it had stopped.

30

After climbing over the car and up the rest of the stairs, I went to work on my ear. Steristrips weren't enough to hold it together, but I found thread and a needle and rubbing alcohol in the first-aid kit. For a second I just stood there, huffing the fumes of the alcohol, wondering if necking it might be the better anaesthetic, but that would only cause me worse bother than I was already in, so I doused my ear and, while the pain was still shrilling, I stuck in the needle and did my best with the thread. My hand needed another top-up, so I found a syringe and jabbed it in.

While I waited for the water to heat up, I undressed and tried to scrub the blood out of my jeans with a toothbrush from the sink. All that did was work up a pinkish foam. The back of my hand was seeping, black, and hurt to rinse, so I wrapped it in a shower-cap, got under the water, stretched the tension out of my back. The sound was like branches snapping. My tongue rasped over the broken corner of my front tooth from where I'd been smacked the day before, and the blood in my piss looked like watermelon juice swirling down the drain, from the rest of that going-over.

A shiver ran through me, and then I wasn't in the shower any more, I was back in Acapulco, in the kitchen of that soldier who I'd interviewed years before, a pitcher of agua de sandía sweating on the table, fan-blades chopping our cigarette-smoke to blue festoons, security lights glowing orange on the banana leaves, the soldier beckoning me in to look at the screen of his phone, where a video showed him slashing at the air with his machete. The speakers hissed with rain. The camera swung around to show six shirtless men on their knees under a tarp, their faces and arms covered in bruises, their mouths stuffed with gym socks, their knees soaked with mud, their eyes huge and white and running with tears.

One of the soldiers jabbed his machete at the piss-stain spreading across the jeans of one of the gagged guys.

'Someone call his mom!' he cackled, then lifted up his machete, swung it into the guy's neck, which burst and fountained.

The camera went back to the other soldiers, who were whaling on the prisoners, the thunk of their machetes wet and constant and dull. A couple of gags slid from a couple of mouths. Their screams buzzed the mic. The rain turned their blood the same pink as the agua de sandía in my glass.

Something hard struck the phone.

'No mames,' laughed the soldier filming, zooming in on a brownish fleck of vertebra lying in the mud.

When the camera went back up again, three heads were on the ground. The top of one man's spine jutted up from the meat of his neck like uncooked ossobuco.

The soldier stopped the video. His breath blew hot and fast on the back of my hand, his hand moving over his scalp, saying, 'The week before that, that gang you see had gotten their hands on a helicopter – don't ask me how. Strafed our barracks. Put holes the size of footballs in the roof, the windows, the walls. Shot my bunkmate to picadillo.' He cracked his knuckles. 'It felt good, what we did. Revenge is a need.'

My heart was a fist thundering against my ribs. That story, I'd worked it alone, because Carlos had gone wandering, said he'd found someone else. Watching the video, I'd pictured myself hacking up this new man of Carlos', had pictured him crying, pleading, had felt my own hurt deepen and sweeten into rage as I pictured the spreading pool of his blood.

Shampoo suds stung my cheek and cut me out of the memory. When I put a finger to the sore spot, something hard was lodged in the skin, and I plucked out a greyish puck of bone, curved like it once had been a part of a skull, and I dropped it, nearly jumped backwards through the shower curtain, but the bone just lay there, gleaming through the suds and the dirt and the blood rinsing off me, until I poked it down the drain with my toe.

Downstairs, there was no noise from the basement. A new smell of burning was in the air, one with a harsh cut of acetylene mixed in, like I knew from my grandfather's workshop. Puccini was sitting at the kitchen table, facing the tank that held Sarabia. In front of him on the table was an open laptop that showed the floorplan of the governor's mansion, the one that we'd stolen in Guatemala City. Beside it, a metal case with a foam inlay sat open beside the laptop. Inside were the kind of metal twists you'd see at a dentist's. A welder's torch and a small gas-canister rested against his knee.

'I take it you finished with him, then,' I said.

Puccini nodded and ran a finger up his middle.

'Blowtorch,' he said.

I waited for a sickened reaction of some kind, but there was nothing.

The laptop rested on a scatter of monochrome photos that had faded to brown shades. He had some printed-out anatomy diagrams there, too, the body parts highlighted in blue, pink and yellow ink, and captioned with bullet-points of cursive handwriting. Some of the photos were of peeled feet being pressed by gloved hands into pools of salt. Other bodies hung nude by the wrists from leather straps tied to basement ceilings.

'War things.' Puccini covered the pictures with an envelope. He pressed his fingers to his eyelids and breathed out in a way that wasn't quite a sigh. 'Manuals, really. We were given them in Fort Bragg. The US got them from the Germans, from their pain-resistance trials on prisoners in the camps.' He waved a hand. 'A rich lineage, all the way to now.'

'Do you want coffee?' I said. 'Because my head is hopping.'

'Please,' said Puccini. 'How's your hand?'

'Oh, you know.' I flexed my fingers, felt my eye twitch. 'Getting used to it.'

'Excellent.'

The sink was full, a steaming, pinkish jelly under clingfilm, and it hissed and bubbled when the condensation dripped back onto it.

'Plastic explosives,' Puccini said, when he caught me peering.

A drop fell sizzling from the clingfilm and I jumped back, startled, but filled up a kettle anyway, set it to boil on the stove. Through the window, I could see ferns nodding in the drench. A magpie hopped past the rainwater that spilled down from the gutter.

'Poor Sarabia,' Puccini said, addressing the tank. He pressed his boot against a loose edge of the skirting-board, lifted his foot away, let the board shake. He folded his arms, fixed his eyes on a knot in the table. 'We were too young for what happened to us. Twelve or so, mostly. They caught Sarabia on his way to play a football game. Standing at a cake-stall. He'd stopped for a treat. At that time, we had these recruiters going around. Anywhere else, they'd just be called kidnapper. Liked the look of him – right shape, right size, whatever. And he was taking a bite of his cake, saw these guys coming, and stuffed the whole thing into his mouth because he thought they wanted the cake.' Puccini clicked his tongue. 'Meant he couldn't scream when they grabbed him. By the time he could, too late, he was on his way to an airfield. Took him all the way to Fort Bragg. Kid had never even been outside his own province.' Puccini pressed his foot against the skirting-board, let it flap loose. 'He wasn't long about getting a drink problem. Thirteen years old, and he's boiling Coke and lighter fluid together to stay going.' Puccini looked up like he had remembered I was there. 'Doesn't destroy you all at once, this stuff,' he said. 'That's the pity of it.'

The kettle shrilled. I killed the gas, poured out two mugs.

'And how'd they get you?' I said, setting his coffee on the table.

Puccini looked at me for a moment. Then he looked at his coffee, his mouth a straight crease, and then he said, 'Nothing explains anything. Whatever I was, I wanted to be the best at it. That's how you stay alive. That's what I was told.' He took a long drink of his coffee and lifted the torture photographs to slide a Maglite torch over to me. A laser was welded in where the bulb had been.

'From the DVD burner,' he said. 'This is for cutting open the windows.' He turned the laptop towards me, scrolled up to a view of the roof, and tapped.

'And I get up there how?'

'The tent-pegs,' he said. 'The brick of the house is porous, as is that of the walls.'

'That looks like a pretty serious fence around the mansion,' I said.

'Rubber gloves and a wire-cutter,' he said. 'Go up half-way, cut from below. Everything will be fine, I will be around the front, making a diversion, so you'll have time. There is a panic room' – he scrolled down, then tapped a boxy shape in the back of a long, top-floor room – 'which is, I think, where the governor will be. So you will take some of the explosive' – he gestured towards the sink – 'and blow this open.'

'There could be a lot of people in the house, man, I don't know.'

Puccini pressed his fingers to his eyelids.

'If you were impressed by what I did here,' he said, 'you have seen nothing yet.'

'And the cameras?'

'We have a jammer. The same one we used at protests, when we worked for the governor. So we know that it's effective.' He drained his coffee, then went to the sink, peeling off the clingfilm and spreading it on the draining-board, before wrapping the immense soapy brick of explosive. 'We should get ready to leave. They may be back.'

Together we walked to the garage. The black jeep that Sarabia had been working on stood at the centre of the garage floor, refitted with so much armour plating that I couldn't tell what shape or make it had been before – the tyres swapped for the fat, off-road kind, the chassis sitting on a raised, four-link suspension like those Dakar rally jeeps. Matter of fact, Sarabia had put a Dakar sticker on the side of the car, along with a whole bunch of other dippy ones – you know the kind, #RESIST, Tibet and Nicaragua and Sri Lanka flags, KANGAROO CROSSING warning triangles – to make it look like the car belonged to some Yank hippie.

'Looks a little too new,' said Puccini, 'but ten minutes on the roads around here, and it'll look just about right.'

'And a white lad behind the wheel,' I said, picking at a SUPPORT OUR TROOPS sticker. 'Nobody will suspect a thing.'

'Can you open the back door?' he said, hefting the brick of explosive.

'Oh. Shit. Yes.' I did as he said, and he leaned in, deposited the brick, then lifted a tarp to reveal a huge assault rifle mounted on a swivel. Belts of cartridges were piled up beside it, with a tablet lying on top. Puccini swiped it unlocked. A gap like a sunroof, except wider, opened above the boot of the jeep. The red LED dot of a GoPro blinked on beside the scope. He traced a circle on the screen with his finger, and the gun swung all the way around.

'A Browning,' Puccini said. 'Army issue.' He knelt at the back of the car, loading stacks of bills – quetzales, pesos, dollars – from a sports-bag into a drawer that pushed out the rear licence plate. He slid a different passport into the gap between each stack, then pushed shut the drawer.

The key was in the ignition when I climbed in. The inside had that new-car smell of formaldehyde and glue, and the vinyl squeaked as I shuffled to get comfy.

'It's like the *Starship Enterprise* in here,' I said to Puccini. 'Height of this thing.'

'Needs to be,' said Puccini. 'No roads where we're going.'

'Jesus.' I pinched the GPS screen out so the whole route showed. 'That's a lot of mountains.'

'Yes. Go around the front, please.'

'What's got this thing so zippy?' I pinged through the options on the GPS, changed the car-icon to a slice of pizza. 'Thought it'd handle like a tank.'

'Boat engine,' said Puccini. 'Park here.'

I stopped us right by the porch. Puccini got out and took a body-bag from the seat behind us. He walked to the porch and pulled it over David's body, then zipped it closed, before reaching into his pocket for a clear plastic baggie that had a load of those clear, contact-lens like bugs inside, before kneeling over the bag and sticking one to the zipper.

'Is that all you're going to do for him?' I said.

'It's more than most bodies get,' he said, and flicked the switch on a tiny radio-transmitter. 'Now, may we?'

'Alright, alright,' I said, and took us cruising past the smoking wreckage, away from the house, and into the fog.

Big trucks and bigger floodwaters had gouged the roads. Driving on that kind of terrain usually made me wish I owned one of those protective cups American footballers used to wear, but the high axle made it feel like I was driving a hovercraft. At the market where we stopped to eat, the air smelled of fresh blood and pine-inspired floor-cleaner. Trolleys clattered, happy kids yawped. Reggaeton and cumbia and old Jeanette songs echoed against the tiles. Parcels of tabloid newspapers lay outside an abarrotes, and I spotted a Facebook photo that I recognised in the top corner of the front page, inside a purple bubble.

'Hey,' I said.

Puccini turned, then looked where I was pointing. His daughter and her boyfriend looked back from that purple bubble on the front page, above a caption that read 'HAVE MERCY ON MY FATHER.'

'Oh,' he said.

'Maya did it.' I bent to slide out a copy of the paper. 'Can't see her liking this particular spin, but you never can control how stuff gets chopped up in syndication.'

'I don't want a copy,' Puccini said, without looking at the stack.

'Oh. OK.' I let go.

We continued on to the comedor. At one of the tables, a man threw back his head to quaff the dregs of his Gallo. For a second, he was one of the cops I'd seen shot. His scalp flapped off, hanging by a red strip of skin, then I blinked and he was just a youngish rancher in a plaid shirt again.

Puccini rapped the table with the second knuckle of his index finger.

'You OK there?' he said.

A Diet Coke that I didn't remember ordering fizzed at my elbow.

Across the restaurant from us sat two secondary-school-age kids, the guy with his arm headlock-tight around the girl's shoulders, the girl with a smile on her face that didn't go all the way to her eyes, his laugh and voice so loud and yappy that I felt sure that if she didn't let him kiss her he'd kill her.

'Nervous, I guess,' I said, taking my eyes from the couple. 'Fuck. I've never raided a house before.' Big ice-cubes clashed in my glass as I lifted it to my lips. 'It's never going to be over, is it?'

Puccini's lips curled downwards, and he bobbed his head, considering the question, then said, 'When they're all dead, and there's no one to prosecute, it all stands a fair chance of being over.'

'Fabulous.' I leaned back against my chair, knuckled my eyes. My head was pitching.

Puccini turned the plastic pages of the menu. Across the floor, a young butcher slung livid garlands of meat on a hook above the counter. The TV was showing a World War II film. I didn't want to look. My foot scuffed against the lino tiles. The marks on one looked like a flaming body.

'This is terrible.' He pointed at the screen. A man lay on a beach, cried for his mother, tried to push his guts back in. 'They never show anything real.'

'Quite sure they can't,' I said. 'Nobody'd join armies otherwise.'

Puccini huffed out another laugh. 'We didn't *join*.'

I mashed some scrambled egg between the tines of my fork. This wasn't something I remembered ordering, either. 'How's the food?'

He sniffed. 'Look, as long as there's red grease leaking out of it, it's probably fine.'

'You say that, but . . .' I held up my burned and broken hand. Puccini ignored me, just wiped his knife and fork with his napkin. 'We should discuss payment.'

Outside the bathroom, an old man wearing a Stetson hat stood in front of the mirror, his hands dripping, as he sighed at his reflection.

'I don't think I want to accept money from you people. I'm in deep enough.'

'Everyone has an owner.' Puccini tore his milanesa in two with a halved tortilla and loaded on salsa roja. 'I told you.'

'You said I could go anywhere. You said I could disappear.'

'And we all need a base.'

'Not a base you know the location of, man.' My fork rattled to the table. People looked. 'C'mon.'

Puccini chewed slowly and swallowed like I wasn't even there, then said, 'We all have associates.'

'I don't know, what do you even want me for?' I shook my head. 'What possible use could I be?' My hand swatted the air. 'Like, you could get literally anyone. That money you have in the jeep, that could buy you any old meathead.'

'And you've seen where any old meathead has gotten us,' he said. 'Or no?'

'Alright, fine, whatever, but – nah, not me, man. Not me.'

'You do have the profile.' He moved on to the other half of his milanesa. 'An alienated white fascinated by violence. A troubled youth. What I perceive to be a family background of intense diligence and equally intense anxiety, on the bottom rung of a given social stratum.'

'Bottom of the middle-classes is still middle-class, man.'

'And it's still the bottom of a social stratum. No, it's fine by me.' He waved a hand. 'Plus, you know, the whiteness, the Spanish, the English. If I ever need you again, you can blur across any border or situation that might be required.' He plucked a tortilla from the pad. 'And I don't anticipate as many dramatics after this, if that proves an enticement.'

'And if everything's over after this, what are you going to need me for? Rebuilding your empire?'

He looked appalled for a second, but then lifted his eyes from the plate.

Puccini, he wasn't really one for looking you in the face – he more just looked *at* you, like you were a thing he was figuring out what to do with.

Right then, though, he wasn't just looking at my eyes – he was looking into them, like he was a normal person.

'To look out for my family,' he said.

Love, if you get this, I know, I know – I should have told him to fuck off, should have told him that if he'd let his people tear what passed for my home and what passed for my family apart, then why the fuck should I keep his together, should have let him drive me into the nearest forest, shoot me, dump me someplace, should maybe even have tried to plug him one myself with the gun I had in my jacket pocket, and for a second my head boiled with all those possibilities, all those options, just this white steam furling and knitting back and forth until the only words in my head were a long ragged scream that no words could ever hope to translate.

But – well, I don't know, it was just the look on his face. That pain, that worry, it plucked me up out of the comedor and dropped me all the way back into the night I'd lost Carlos, back into my steel-frame Frankfurt chair, back beside the fever-pallor on the shrines where I'd lit candles to bribe my saints, back under the dim green glow of lamps through the giraffe orchids and begonias and ferns of my indoor garden, while my cupped hands held the faces of all the people I'd interviewed about the loved ones they'd lost, and while my chest held an ache that has never truly faded.

It's like I told you before, about the mutant heart thudding away inside me, turned to leather by air pollution and a bad life, hardened in the short term, but just about clapped out, too. Well, if you're like me, and you have a blackened nub like that in you, pumping nothing but poison, you really do just want some kind of redemption to come at you from somewhere, and you'll grab at whatever chance of that there is, no matter where it's coming from, no matter who, and so I don't know, maybe that's why I didn't do any of those things I should have, and maybe that's why I just shrugged, looked back at my cooling eggs, my flat Diet Coke, and said, 'Ah. Yeah, OK. Whatever.'

'Thank you, Andrew. I'm grateful.'

The woman running the comedor swooped in for my plate. I put on my sunglasses.

'Couldn't handle that salsa, could he?' she said, laughing a little at me. 'Look at those eyes water.'

'It would seem so,' Puccini said, and paid.

32

Thick fog broke over the bonnet, making the windscreen shine. Shrubs and low trees whapped the undercarriage of the jeep. We'd been driving for hours, the trees either side thickening to forest, the road tapering to a single lane, then a muck track spined with grass, until we were weaving through pine and balsam trees, and until the pizza-slice icon on the GPS was nudging the chequered flag marked 'LA FAENA'. My eyes felt baked in their sockets. Wind rushed the branches and shredded the headlit fog into rags. In the back seat, Puccini was cutting the block of plastic explosives into fat rectangles, wrapping them in clingfilm, and wrapping each cut brick with a tress of rope that smelled like it had been soaked in tar. Only a narrow gulley stood between us and the mansion. The green of the ferns was so vivid that it nearly hissed, the same tint as the Mexico photos from the encyclopaedias at my grandfather's house.

'We're within range now,' Puccini said quietly. 'You can pull in.'

When I did, I sat there with my hand pressed to the bulge of Carlos' ashes. My other hand fumbled in the pocket that held his old PRESNA lanyard. The air through the open window smelled coolly of loam.

Puccini had finished stacking the bricks. Now he was reaching boxes of drones into the seat with him.

'How many of these did you buy?'

'You won't be shocked if I admit I didn't pay for them, given everything, I'm sure.' He handed me a box. 'If you could?'

'Twelve of them. Jesus. How did you cart all that out?'

'There was time, in the end. I hid in the meat-fridge.'

'And you didn't think to bring your beloved fucking colleagues with you, no?'

He stopped assembling the drone and looked at me, a Stanley knife in his hand.

'Alright, alright,' I said, and popped open the box.

As we put the drones together, we laid them outside the car. They were the small, bony kind, light white plastic frames that look like they'll break if you glance at them sideways, but that didn't stop Puccini from strapping two bricks of plastic explosive to each one before putting the remaining bricks in a blue canvas tote bag. Once that was loaded, he took out his laptop computer and opened it up. A program I didn't recognise was running, a black rectangle at the centre of the screen, and he typed in a command and the drones began to power up, whirring lightly. As they did, tiny squares began to appear in the central rectangle, showing a view from each camera. The laptop was a touch-screen, so he tapped on one of the squares and lifted a drone into the air with the arrow-keys, and I watched the view from the camera swing up through the trees and into the dark air, towards the governor's mansion. The camera showed only one man patrolling the outside, and he seemed to be having a cheeky smoke with his headphones on, because he didn't look up as the drone whizzed past overhead.

'That should make it easy for you, then,' Puccini said. 'Just one to worry about.'

The grounds blurred past – the brick wall capped with razor-wire, the blot-shaped lake, the lush gardens and loaded trellis, the triangular privets, the mossy statues of Cortés and La Malinche, their cheeks and eyes and the gaps between their fingers climbed black with rain-carried dirt. Five police Camrys and six jeeps were parked outside the house, along with a helicopter. Nobody was on patrol outside, apart from a pair of men at each door – on the L-shaped roof terrace by the pool, at both side doors, and at the front and back.

'You see here?' Puccini let the drone hover for a moment. He ran a finger along the screen, between the wall of the house and the perimeter wall. 'This is the widest stretch of wall between doors. So you climb here, you cut through the garden, cross this bit of lawn, and climb the trellis to the window.'

Hearing all this was like standing on the edge of a diving board.

'When you cut through the window, the floorplan tells me that you'll be in a monitoring room. If there's personnel, get rid of them.' He handed me a brick of plastic explosive. 'Just an ordinary Zippo to light it.'

All I could feel was the air in my nostrils, the pre-heart-attack stutter of my blood.

'The panic room is at the bottom of the corridor.' He tapped up an image of the floorplan. 'Blow it open and wait for me. I'll attract the remainder of the personnel.'

He pressed a command. The view through the camera spun as it plummeted, enough to give me vertigo just watching, and the last thing the camera caught was the soaked muck of the ground bursting, like a pot of stew wobbled by bubbles. From where we were sitting, the blast was a deep thud of somebody whacking a pint glass with the flat of their hand. A couple of cries echoed through the dark.

'Good,' Puccini said. He typed in another command and the rest of the drones rose into the air at once, forming up into a V and scudding towards the mansion. Their cameras lit up the black rectangle into tiny squares.

'How's that meant to work?'

'You can get them to home in on the nearest WiFi router,' he said. 'It's a simple thing to do.'

The first drone caught the helicopter on its way down, an explosion that lit the sky, while the other drones' cameras showed flying glass, sharded metal, and a man flying through the air in an awkward backflip, landing with his limbs all twisted up like a swastika.

'You can override them, too,' Puccini said, tapping on a square, and flying the drone down into the bonnet of one of the jeeps. Around the edges of the view I saw men in black crouched in the doorway, firing upwards. The sound fritzed the speakers with static, and the echo popped and rattled through the dark.

'We might be near a safe moment for you to go,' Puccini said, minimising the program as the chain of drones began paying itself forward through the blown-open window of the mansion, and opening another that showed a map of where we were from above. A cluster of red dots blinked on and off.

'This indicates all the devices that are active in the area,' he said, then got to his feet and got out of the car. I did the same thing, and followed him around to the boot. He opened it and took out a blue metal box with a small circular aerial affixed to the top of it. He rested this on the bonnet, aimed the aerial towards the mansion, and pressed a button that made two small green lights flicker into life.

'That the jammer?'

He nodded.

I went around to the boot and fetched a pair of long-handled wire-cutters, fastened the tool into place across the top of my backpack, then pulled one of the rubber gloves on over my good hand.

At the front of the car, the jammer's aerial turned with a light whirring sound. One by one the cluster of red dots began to flicker and blink until there were none.

The explosions had finished rocking the house. Now engines turned over, people shouted orders, and lights flared beyond the walls of the mansion.

'Your route,' Puccini said, clicking something that fleshed out the map until it looked like a satellite photo. 'Seventy-eight paces this way, yes?' He pointed. 'No more, no less.

Then you go, what, three hundred paces towards the stream. You can see the bridge here, no? And beyond that the wall. We have knocked out the electric fence, so you can cut through without a problem, climb over on those tent-pegs, and then cut directly in front of you to the wall of the house.'

'Then the trellis,' I said. There was no shake in my voice, but I felt like I'd been packed from hip to rib with ice.

'If you're seen,' Puccini said, and handed me the tote bag of explosive bricks, 'you know what to do. And don't forget these.' He dropped a pair of earplugs into my open palm, then climbed into the jeep and drove off in a curve, towards the noise of revving engines. My breath felt like it was only filling the tops of my lungs. For a second I thought about making a break for it, back the way we'd come, but I couldn't re-member the last time we'd passed a house, and, besides, what would I even say? All I could do was go the way that Puccini had showed me – forward, into the dark.

33

Stalking through the dark, jumping at every sound, I made my way as far as the clearing near the bridge. When a fat rat scarpered across in front of me I nearly blew it away.

Cicadas pulsed. Birds yawked. The rain smell on everything was like your hair after your trips to the gym. Overhead, the stars were a tiny, smashed-glass glitter.

The clearing led uphill through the pines, past resin-stained, moisture-darkened rocks, towards a noise of water, and there was the bridge, above a spate of white water and black rocks. A couple of planks were missing and the wooden rail was rotted and slick with moss. The best thing was to try to gallop across it, I reckoned, until I actually did try to gallop across it, and wound up putting my foot through one plank, soaking my whole leg, and whacking my ankle against a rock before falling, shoulder-first, into the marshy ground of the far side, where I lay, half-winded, until I could move again.

When I got my breath back, the smell hit me.

It's like I told you – death has a dozen smells, and I only know some.

But the ones I do know, I can't forget.

The calcified dead, smoking in a burned-out car, they're diesel oil and burned skin.

The hog-tied dead, dumped on beaches, the sweetish cloy of their blood impossible to tell apart from the odour of parching seaweed.

And the dead of the mass-graves – deep, fungal, butanoic.

And that was the smell that was all over me, all over my shoulders and chest, my feet and my legs.

When I put my hand down to push myself up, I felt eels of muddied hair slick between my fingers. My knees bumped a skull. My feet pressed hard on a stretch of skin and I felt it give way. When I looked around, I saw how bumpy the ground was, how purple with rot the muck had gone around the river. Who those people were, I have no idea, but they'd rotted enough to date from the time when Puccini was working for the governor. They could have been anyone – people like Carlos, people like the women on the MISSING posters on every lamp-post in Poza Rica, people like Julián Gallardo, people like the ones in the photos Maya and I had seen on the railings of the Congreso.

A flare of orange reared up with a *boom* somewhere in the forest. Tyres skirled. A scooter engine whined. Guns went off – big ones, small ones. My eyes moved along the treeline as far as the mansion. The eaves of the house looked like they were frowning. For a second it was like the house had made those bodies, all by itself, just leaking them into the dirt. Every deal, every bargain, every favour for every Roberto Zúñiga, every bought cop, every Puccini, it all led to this marsh. Every dead activist, every dead Carlos, every missing person who'd never come home, the money that had killed them was the same money that had paid for those walls, the same money that was keeping the governor alive in there, afloat on that lake of blood-thickened muck.

Something came flaming through the trees, whipping end over end in circles, crashing through the little copse of birch saplings that had been planted in the surface of the grave, and sank itself hissing into the wet earth near where I stood. The flames lit up the back of a scooter.

A torch cut through the dark, over by the wall, landing on the scooter, then tracked left, lit me up.

'Hey,' said a man's voice. I heard boots start to squelch towards me. 'We've warned you people. Don't be coming around here.'

'Oh, hello.' I gave him a stupid wave, added a bashful little chuckle to my voice, then took Carlos' press lanyard from his pocket. 'Press, actually. International. We wanted to have an interview with the governor?'

'What the fuck?' the gunman said. Muzzle of his rifle came up. The flashlight glared in my face. 'You – get out!'

'It's just a few words.' I walked towards him. My boots were full of rot, my shins soaked with it. He was less than ten yards away.

'Hey, man, relax, this is private property,' he said. 'We don't want anyone here. Just turn around.'

Now he was within reach of me.

'Hey! I said turn around! Don't make me shoot you!'

'Oh, God!' I screamed, acting like I'd suddenly seen all the black dirt on me. 'Oh, where am I? What am I standing in?' I staggered forward, let myself stumble.

'Just relax,' he said, sounding nervous. 'Just turn around and walk.'

'Oh no, oh no!' I kept up the screaming, then let myself fall, face-first, towards him, against his chest, and then I pulled the trigger of the gun in my pocket – once, twice, three times – and the guard staggered away from me in a pink cloud, the strap of his rifle sliding from his shoulder and wrapping his forearm. He tottered backwards and his head clunked against a rock. Smoke was pouring from my pocket. A little flame had bloomed up at the corner of Carlos' jacket, so I clapped it out, then dragged the body by the feet into the mud, before heading for the wall. The noise of the fight was nearer the house now – loud booms, yells, the hiss of flares, the rattle of automatic fire. A violet flare lit the night.

The brick was porous enough to hammer in the first pair of tent-pegs, even with my hand as knackered as it was. Two more put me head-height below the bale of wire, and I reached the cutters from the bag behind me and set to work, the coils winking as they dropped past my head onto the grass. Once it looked to me like there was enough space, I tapped in another couple of tent-pegs, climbed the rest of the way, and peeped over the top, so low to the wire that my chin scraped the edges of the broken glass glued to the top. Nobody was standing beside either door – they must all be at the front, trying to repel Puccini – so I hammered in two more tent-pegs, wobbled a bit as I climbed onto them, and kicked myself as far above the wall as I could, landing just past the lotus-flower-shaped metal spines hidden in the hedges closest to the wall. The thud left me winded, my arms hugged across my chest so the bag of Carlos' ashes wouldn't burst.

After scuttling towards the wall of the house, I ducked below a sill and slipped across to the trellis. A dead camera hung nodding from the eave. The burn and cuts on the back of my hand had opened. Drops of blood pattered on the ivy leaves as I went, hauling myself above the gutter onto the roof-tiles. The dew made them slippery, but I'd been climbing stupidly tall things since I was a teenager – quarry walls, car parks, all the places you go when there's nothing to do around where you're growing up.

From the roof, I could see Puccini's headlights cutting through the dark. Thick plumes of smoke were rising from where he'd been. About eight men in black combat gear were running ahead of him, but the Browning was up and swinging, purple tracer-fire cutting the dark, and the ones he didn't shoot down, he just ran down. Soon his headlights were lighting up the spikes of the gate, and the sound of running feet and yelled orders was everywhere below me in the house. Directly beneath, though, through the skylight was a wide, wood-beamed room with a bank of monitors in the corner, the screens showing teems of static, pixelated nothings, frozen loading bars, and those rainbow wheels that a Mac shows when it's fucked. It seemed safe enough to take out that Maglite-laser thing Puccini had given me and try it on the glass. The rose-coloured line hummed and traced a smoking rectangle in the glass, enough for a bit of elbow pressure to knock it through to the carpet below, and I let myself drop onto the carpet, the draught of my fall shaking a Noguchi light fixture that hung from the ceiling.

The walls were fir-panelled, their varnish the colour of amber, and the carpet was so thick and new and white that it could have been the plush outsides of a polar-bear teddy. Moonlight whitened the dust-motes.

Instead of a door, they'd put in a paper screen with balsa-wood frames, and I watched shadows go running past, heard yells, curses, people cocking guns. When I was sure all of them had gone past, I slid the screen open and tip-toed out-side, my back pressed to the wall. The rooms off the rest of the corridor had those screens, too, and the walls were papered in yellow, decorated with bridges and red and blue dragons and people dressed in Japanese costumes. A samurai sword in a scabbard rested on two ivory pegs.

Eight or nine men were mobbed on a raised balcony that looked down on the lower floor, firing downwards at the front window. The bass rumble of an engine grew louder, nearing them, and then there was a crash of glass and a white flare of headlights. That was when I stopped watching, and kept going towards the panic room on the top floor. After laying the wrapped explosives in a line across the bottom, I pulled out their fuses, lit them, and backed into the room next to it, twisting first one earplug and then the other into my ears as sparks fizzed along the fuse. One man turned and lifted his gun at me, but there was the crump of a shot, a little puff of wood coughed from the banister nearest him, and he dropped in a red cloud of blood. There was a sucking boom that nearly lifted the top of my head off. Splinters shredded the carpet. All the noises went wobbly and underwater – gunshots became bubbles bursting, people's yells became the lowing of cows, and everything was edged by a high tingling sound that hurt my eardrums. Heads turned on the balcony, and guns came up, but then a drone fell towards them in a plume of purple smoke, and I heard screams and a boom and didn't stick around to see what had happened to them, just forward-rolled through the gap blasted in the door's layers of metal and wood, then flattened myself around the corner, and looked up to see Governor Janiel Uruchurtu sitting in a yellow silk kimono patterned like the wallpaper outside, zip-tied by the wrists and ankles to an office-chair, a cross of gaffer-tape over his mouth, his glasses cracked, the dye greying from his hair. His forehead creased with hope when he saw me, his body strained towards me, and little anxious mutters reached me through the gag.

The shooting had stopped. The groaning had not. A jeep door slammed downstairs. Footsteps clinked through what sounded like a thick layer of smashed glass and scattered cartridges. Three sharp, silenced pops stopped the groans.

The footsteps grew nearer. Someone shuffled on the balcony, I heard broken-jawed pleading that was cut short by a wet thud, and then there Puccini stood in the flaming doorway, his vest and face stained black, his arms gloved with red, the samurai sword in one hand, a handgun in the other.

The governor screamed into the tape over his mouth.

'Why'd they tape him up?' I said.

'Because he's a fucking coward,' said Puccini. 'And he'd only run around screaming, get himself killed.' He looked at the governor and said, 'This reminds me of the battalion. Of Mass.'

The governor's feet kicked.

'The bishops,' Puccini said, 'they'd tell us about the Gospel.' He took a metal case from the bandolier across his chest and clicked it open. 'They'd tell us about the parable of the camel passing through the eye of the needle.'

The governor's office-chair rolled backwards, then fell over.

Puccini took a needle from the foam casing inside the box and tested the point on his finger. The governor's eyes were wild in their sockets, locked on the shine of that needle.

'The bishops,' said Puccini, 'told us that the poor read the story all wrong. They thought that the eye of the needle was the gate to heaven, but really it was the gate to the city, and that the rich man was a thief, his camel loaded with things stolen from the righteous.'

The governor pulled his head away. His tortoiseshell glasses tipped onto the floor. Sobs wracked his body.

Puccini knelt beside the body and held the eye of the needle over the governor's eyes.

'Now the bishops,' Puccini said, 'they told us that the Communists were those thieves, and that our battalion was the watchtower. But now I know it's different.' He rapped the governor's nose with the hoop around the eye of the needle and laughed gently when the governor flinched.

'It's the rich man who's the thief,' Puccini said, 'and I am the watchtower.'

The governor's face was soaked with tears. A patch of wet spread on the carpet, and I felt a dark joy ripple upwards through me from the pit of my stomach as I took the bag of Carlos' ashes from inside my jacket pocket so that Carlos could watch.

Puccini turned at the noise of the bag hitting the floor, and looked at me like he'd forgotten I was there.

'Could you go downstairs,' Puccini said, 'and get me some salt? For his feet, you see.'

'Sure.' I got to my feet and made for the stairs.

'Thank you.' Puccini leaned forward. I didn't see what he was doing, but I heard the governor's muffled scream against the tape.

The stairs were a mess. A body was still kicking on the balcony. Another lay stuck through the banisters of the upper deck, the bottom of his leg dangling by a tendon. Once again, Puccini had crashed the jeep through the front window. Smoke from the muzzle of the Browning trailed over the roof and bonnet. Two torched jeeps and a helicopter smoked in the driveway. The rest of them didn't bear looking at, but there was nothing I could do against the smell except go downstairs with a hand over my mouth.

Even through the wreckage, you could see the opulence of the place – white leather sofas, armchairs on liquid-looking metal stalks, a 50-inch flatscreen, animal skins on the floor, Mayan lootings in glass cases. Mingled in were kinetic art pieces that looked like originals by Ed Ruscha and Victor

Vasarely and Denise René – spirals of black card, dots of bright colours that looked like brake lights in the rain, stuff like that. Patches of carpet were in flames from the chunks of styrofoam flung everywhere. All of it was shattered now, all of it scarred with burns.

Even half shot to shit, the kitchen was a dream. The sink was stone, the stove was cast-iron, huge clay pots hung from the walls, and the table was capped in white enamel. The coffee I found in the freezer smelled past its best, but whatever, there was a fancy box of pink rock salt in one of the presses. After taping paper towels over the backs of my burned hand, I got some bottles of Evian out of the fridge and started to make coffee. It was only when I turned on the taps and couldn't hear the sound of the water that I realised how loudly my ears were ringing. While the water boiled, I went to the jeep, to rescue the last donuts left in my seabag. As I did, though, the mattress-needle Maya had found in the elephant candle fell out of one of the compartments inside, and landed right in my hand. I brought it inside with me, microwaved the donuts, then I filled a French press, fetched two cups and a tray, loaded on the water and the donuts and the mattress-needle and the salt, then walked up the blackened steps and back to Puccini and the governor in the panic room.

34

What we did to the governor, how much I helped – well, love, if you get this, some things it's better I don't tell you.

My brain felt like it had been microwaved afterwards. As we staggered down the stairs, past the smoking bodies, Puccini offered me his water but I shook my head and just zombied my way down through the kitchen to the L-shaped terrace by the pool, and let myself drop onto one of the couches there beside the fireplace, my ass crunching onto the curls of dried leaves that had settled in the folds of the cushions. Moths teemed the sensor-lights, and all I could think of was snow over El Paso, a blizzard over Uruguay. A black trash of pine-needles and dirt and dead insects turned on the surface of the pool, became starlings in high blue air, the swirl of yerba maté in boiling water.

A router blinked beside the fireplace, and I got the code from it, turned on my phone, sent Maya a pin with my location. As the phone began to buzz with all the missed calls and texts from the last couple of days, I dropped it onto the table, beside the pistol that I was completely sick of feeling dig into the small of my back.

No messages from you waited for me on my phone, but there was a missed call from Sancho, so I went out to the terrace to call him back.

'My man,' he said, when he picked up. 'You OK? You relapse or something?'

'Ah, I did and I didn't,' I said. 'Be less complicated if I had just gone and picked up, to be fair.'

'The old dry-drunk,' said Sancho.

'Yeah. Stupid shit. Codependency. Adrenaline. Sugar. Danger.' I kicked a heap of leaves that had gathered by the wall. 'Bad form all round.'

Sancho laughed sadly and said, 'Oh, I know it well.'

'Figured there was a reason you sold me the car. Speaking of which' – I lit a Bali with the Zippo I'd taken from the floor of Sarabia's basement – 'I've returned it to you. The car, I mean.'

'Oh?'

'It's at a private hangar near Ezeiza,' I said. 'I'll send you the location. All the papers are in your name still, so you just show up. Long-stay parking.'

'So you won't be back at the group, then.'

'No,' I said, 'but this isn't a geographic cure, like – don't worry.'

Sancho tutted. 'Look, I mean, it's sad to lose you, but if you're sure you're dry et cetera . . .'

'Yeah.' The cigarette was making my hand shake. 'Find a group, do the steps, don't be a dick. You mind if I call you back?' I said. My fingers were pressed to my eyelids. They smelled like ash and seared minerals. 'Stuff to do here.'

'Same,' said Sancho. He sounded disappointed. I didn't blame him. 'But you give me a call when you're settled.'

'Sure thing. Lots of love.'

Turning the gun on the wrought iron, watching the pool, wishing it was the one I'd sat beside years ago, I felt myself wishing it was years ago, wishing that Helen would come pelting out of the house to throw herself into the sunlit water, the splash flying up to patter on the white nieve de Morelos blossoms.

Puccini stayed inside for a long time, clanking and hammering away at something. After a while he came back out and stood with his back to me by the pool, his combat jacket back on against the cold.

'My lawyer made you the owner of a bar in Honduras,' he said. 'She also made a bank account for you.'

'Problematic,' I said, and lifted my six-month chip on its keyring, then went back to spinning the gun in circles against the metal – away from Puccini, towards Puccini.

He took a drag of smoke. 'There is no bar, of course – it's just a house. But your payment will be registered as its profits, and she will handle any tax issues. The arrangement is locked in, no matter what happens. There are understandings for foreigners in Honduras who own property relating to tourism, you see.'

'Would that be it?'

Towards Puccini, away from Puccini.

'What do you mean?'

'As in, no more word from you, no more jobs, no more calls.'

Geckoes pattered over the concrete. The sky was a sheet of fog. All I could hear was the rain, my breath, the creak of moss-coated oaks beyond the wall.

Away from Puccini, towards Puccini.

He turned around, a rueful look on his face, but all I could see when I looked at him was the purple mud of that mass grave beyond the wall.

Bats strafed midges through the dark-blue air.

Towards Puccini, away from Puccini.

'Oh, Andrew, we've been through that,' he said. 'It might only be periodically. But in case of emergency, you never know.'

'Right.'

My hand stopped turning the gun.

The sun was above the treeline now, reddening little white scuts of cloud, turning the rimrock behind the house pink.

'I guess that's as good as it gets,' I said.

'Well, not quite.' He reached into the pocket of his cargo pants and dropped an Irish passport onto the table.

My stomach turned to water. Stuck to the front of the passport was a lilac Post-It taken from the block of them beside the governor's kitchen sink. 'Take the jeep here. Ask for Walter. He owns the plot we're pretending you're renting.' Puccini buttoned up his jacket. 'The lot is on AirBnB as a permanently block-booked location. That's how we pay for his silence.'

'And I can stay there?'

'That would be the idea, yes,' he said.

It was a perfect copy – biometric, the paper the right weight, the red and the gold pristine. There's no point telling you what name there was inside it, but the photo was mine.

'Wow,' I said, flicking the pages. 'Completely unspoiled.'

'You're nowhere now,' Puccini said. 'A ghost.'

I pocketed the passport.

He slid back the sleeve of his combat jacket, checking his watch. 'Well, I think our time's at an end.'

'Just one thing, though.' I ran a finger across my fingers. 'How did you wind up a United fan?'

'I'm not.' He looked down at the 'MUFC' tattoo inked across his knuckles, so old that the black was nearly green.

The gun was under my hand again now.

Towards Puccini, away from Puccini.

'I lost a bet. 1999. Bayern Munich. Sarabia's idea. Because I told him there was no way they would come back from that.' He was looking at his knuckles, smiling a little. 'What a character. So hard to lose one like him. But so hard to keep them all safe from us, you know? From other people. From ourselves.'

Love, if you get this, it's like I told you before – you want to hurt someone, remind them of what they lost.

'I know one way.'

Away from Puccini, towards Puccini.

'Yes, well, of course, there are always two options, in any situation,' Puccini said, 'because one of them is always death.'

Towards Puccini, away from Puccini.

He looked out over the pool, at the light dripping glycerine orange from the palm-trees. He was as calm as I'd ever seen him, and I gritted my teeth, tasted the air above that purple muck at the back of the mansion – all that rot, all that cancelled life, all of the death that he'd been a part of since before I'd even been born.

'Pretty dark, man,' I said.

Away from Puccini, towards Puccini.

He laughed.

'Oh, you know what it's like,' he said. 'How damage can turn you strange.'

My breath felt like steam shooting in and out of my nose.

'I mean, you've lost everything, too – home, twice, family, twice, friends – everything.'

'Yeah, and my cat,' I heard myself say.

He had time to turn around, and he had time to look puzzled, like he wasn't sure if I was joking. He even had time to reach for his gun when he saw mine, but he had no more time than that. My first shot caught him in the centre of that scar bisecting his face. My second caught him in the chest, between the third and fourth rib, destroying the heart completely. The rest of the shots, I don't remember, but he was in the pool and my finger hurt and the gun had been clicking for what felt like a long time when I stopped pumping the trigger at last and walked to the edge of the pool to look down at him there, floating cruciform below the surface, under a cloud of blood so dark that it almost looked purple. His eyes didn't look any different to when he'd been alive.

There was one car intact out front, a black Camry. I went back around, got the net for cleaning the pool out of the corner, and drew Puccini by the ankle towards the steps. A thick gout of blood and water splashed onto the concrete as I dragged him out. I pulled him by the ankles all the way through the house to the driveway where it was parked, opened the boot, then lifted him in. My back ran with sweat, and my heart was going ninety. It was like hauling railway sleepers around the gardens I'd landscape with my father, just that dense, boring weight. I took the bugs and the radio transmitters from one of his pockets, but the rest of what he had, I didn't care about it. The keys were still in the ignition. After that I drove him through the grounds of the mansion, past the white plastic greenhouses, past the maze, past a terraced staircase of rock that I'd read in the papers had been stolen from the pyramid at Tajín, all the way to the rim of the black lake that I'd seen at the top of the map, then parked with the nose facing the water, got out, and took a rock from the grass to weigh the accelerator down. The car rolled down the slope, hit the water with a splash, and began to sink with a thick bubbling sound. I watched until the last bubble broke the surface. I didn't say anything. I just put my sunglasses on and walked back to the house. The governor's fridge contained mostly luxury meats and cheeses that were the dank, bluish kind whose taste always put the smell of mass graves back on my palate, meaning I settled for beans, rice, tortillas, fried plantains. The bandage was sopping on my wrecked hand, so I tore it off, went to get some Superglue from the jeep, and stuck the edges of the cuts together. As I fried, the light whitened the crazing of dried glue holding shut the back of my hand. I stood at the bullet-holed stove, ate from the pans, watched clouds dissolve above the hills.

After breakfast, I found some zip-ties in the jeep, shut the boot on myself, then, with my teeth, I pulled the zip-ties shut around my wrists and ankles, straining so hard that my knees nearly popped, before tearing off a strip of gaffer-tape and pressing it over my mouth. After that I just lay there, waiting for the sirens, counting back from forty, holding on to the sound of the numbers as they rose and burst in my head, because they were the only thing I could think of that wouldn't bring the bad pictures of everything that had happened. How close to zero I got, I don't know, but it wasn't long before the sleep came rolling in, as thick and black as smoke.

35

The click of the boot opening woke me, and I found myself looking up into the face of Sandra, David's colleague.

'Where's David?' she said, ripping the gaffer tape off my mouth.

The raw pain made a blank of my head for a second. I opened and shut my mouth a couple of times. A whole load of stubble had come away on the tape. It hurt to look at the little caught hairs.

'My pocket,' I said.

She stepped back, looking at me like I was crazy.

'No, no,' I said. 'A transmitter. With his location.' I rolled and jerked my head. 'Just turn it on.'

She closed her eyes.

'How?' she said. There was a rhythmic shake in her jaw.

'I didn't see,' I said, because that seemed like the kind option.

She put her fingers in my pocket, took out the transmitter, and pressed the button. A little strip of screen like on a calculator lit up, showing the coordinates of Sarabia's place.

She nodded and walked away, towards the house. Inside, paramedics were busy zipping the bodies into bags, labelling bagged parts, some drawing chalk outlines, others lifting bodies. Red and blue lights flickered over the carpet.

Maya walked out of the front doorway, a hand over her mouth and nose.

'You could have told me to bring a dental mask or something,' she said when she saw me, wafting a hand before her face.

'You get used to it.' I lifted my hands. 'Could you? There's a Stanley knife in the jeep somewhere.'

Maya looked at my hands. 'Oh, fuck. What happened?'

'Four new knuckles. I'll never write again.' With my fists I swatted a bluebottle from my ear, which throbbed, and was still leaking. My broken hand was throbbing away too, but, with everything else going on, that pain was a ground-bass that I could kind of tune out.

'That hand will heal, Andrew.' Maya opened the back door of the jeep and started looking through the pieces. 'You'll be able to type for sure.'

'Maybe, but I'm not taking any chances.'

'Jesus, what is all this stuff? It's like a factory in here.' Puccini had stripped off the armour and dismounted the gun, but the rest must have still been lying around.

'I don't know,' I said. 'I was tied up and unconscious for all of it.'

'Yeah, right.' She walked back around to the boot, snicked through the ties with the tip of the Stanley knife. 'No mames, I think your ear is going to make me sick.'

'Ankles, too, please.'

'Alright, alright.'

'Mighty kind of you.' I swung my legs from the boot, got out, and stretched. 'How's it looking in there?'

'You tell me,' Maya said, then slapped her forehead. 'Oh, wait! You were miraculously unconscious. I forgot.'

'That's the spirit.'

We walked inside. From the sitting room, I could see where two uniformed police stood by the door to the panic room. Sandra was standing on the terrace, her phone held to her ear.

'You got here fast,' I said.

'We were already on the way,' Maya said. 'I found that fucking bug you put on my Citalopram.'

'Oh.'

'Yeah. Then one of the police nerds reverse programmed it. Still had to bargain my way onto the helicopter, though, didn't I?'

'You get photos upstairs?'

'Enough,' Maya said.

'So, one, then.'

'Yeah.' She lifted the pan from the stove. 'Oh, wow. You even cooked while unconscious.'

'You hungry or anything?' I said, scraping the leftovers from the pans into some Tupperware that I'd found under the sink.

'Ah. No, Andrew. I'm OK.'

'Stomach feeling a bit rough after the flight?'

'Sure,' she said. 'That's why.'

Sandra was brushing black leaf-dust from the couch. Her face was red.

Maya tutted, said, 'She was shouting at the cops' press people on the helicopter. Saying they should put "killed in action" instead of "called from this life".'

'She knew, then.' I filled two glasses of water at the sink, got ice from the dispenser attached to the fridge.

'She didn't.' Maya took the glass I handed her. 'But she could guess how it was going to turn out.'

The forensics people were snapping photos of the carpet stains now, and laying numbered plastic plates over the spent cartridges. On the terrace, a policeman in uniform was nodding to a string of orders from Sandra, his notepad held over his crotch.

Upstairs, the panic-room door opened. A plainclothes policeman walked out, coughing, a handkerchief pressed to his mouth.

'You sleep through that, too?' Maya said.

'Ah.' I spun the Fidel Castro keyring around my finger. I'd clipped on the keys to the jeep. 'Kind of.'

'If anyone deserved that,' Maya said, watching as the stretcher with the sheet over it came downstairs, 'it was probably the governor. Where'd the other guy go?'

'No idea.'

She looked at me sidelong.

Love, if you get this, it's like I told you. I never could get anything past Maya.

'No chingues, güey,' she said. 'What the fuck happened to you?'

239

The ice-cube in my glass was the shape of Uruguay, so I poured it into my mouth, gnashed it to pieces, let the melt-water numb my throat.

'What now, then? Where do you think you'll go?' Maya said. 'Back home?'

My foot scuffed an ash-stain on the tile.

'You have that little donut wallet on you?' I said.

She squinted at me.

'Why?'

'Present for you.'

She shielded her handbag from me.

'What kind?'

'Just get it out for me, will you?'

'Alright, alright.' She rooted out the little wallet. 'You going to spike me or some shit?'

'In a manner of speaking.' I reached into my pocket and took out the last radio transmitter. 'Switch this on in a week or so. Come for a holiday. Or else just sack it off, move on down.'

Maya looked at the little transmitter.

'What do you say?' I said. 'You and me, iguana-brained with heat, a chaste sham marriage, swapping one kind of late-life angst for another.'

'Yeah, alright.' Maya zipped up the wallet and dropped it into her handbag. 'That sounds, like, twenty-five per cent OK.'

'I like those odds,' I said, and drained my glass.

Now Sandra strode in from the terrace.

'This is a real mess,' she said, her hand stroking her chin. Her eyes were puffy from crying. 'My superiors agree. And we think it might be best if you just disappear.' Her other hand gripped her elbow. The knuckles whitened. 'Don't you?'

'Yeah. I think so.' I took David's wallet out of my pocket and handed it to her. She didn't say anything. I went to collect my Tupperware, then Maya went with me to the jeep. As I was opening the door, she gave me a hug that felt more like a rugby tackle.

'Ow, watch the hand,' I said, as I sat backwards into the jeep.

'That was on purpose,' said Maya.

'Typical,' I said. 'So, that holiday, then?'

'Long as you don't fuck it up, yeah? Like the last one.' Maya was looking back at the house. 'This whole thing was horrific.'

'Love you, too.' I shut the door, reversed the car over the rubble. Maya waved me off as I drove past the wreck left in the driveway, and then she, too, was lost in the fog.

36

Labourers in orange overalls were hosing off the road. The ash and burned engine-parts, the blood, they could have been from anything – a pile-up, an overturned lorry, whatever. Probably that was the idea behind getting it all cleaned up so fast, I guess.

Driving all night took me to the border with Honduras. Nothing much was in the papers or on the TV beyond 'shoot-out at forest residence, fugitive governor believed to be among the dead.' Maya's story had some extra pictures, but not many extra details. The foreign journalists were all tweeting wire-service stuff, or paraphrasing the local papers, so it would be a while before the truth filtered out.

A nurse sewed my ear up and took care of my hand at a pharmacy-cum-clinic, then I ate from my Tupperware while sitting on the jeep-bonnet, went for a walk towards a church dedicated to Maximón that stood on the main square. Outside the church, a couple of bakers were getting their shop consecrated by a priest wearing a purple bandana. They'd laid a ring of loaves and eggs around a heap of grains, seeds, and apples, then capped the whole thing with a photo of their bakery. The priest knelt to the loaves, a lit taper of newspaper in his hand, while a guitar trio serenaded the blaze with a song about largesse, suffering, protection.

The couple smiled and nodded at my approach. The Maximón statuette they held between them was dolled up like a gang boss, black suit, red tie, his moustache as pristine as Pedro Infante's. The priest was kneeling before them, muttering a prayer that I couldn't decipher.

The loaves blackened and popped in the fire, and I flinched at each bursting sound. As the priest rose to his feet, blowing smoke from a stuffed and folded tobacco-leaf over the couple and the statuette and the fire, one of the eggs exploded, flinging shreds of a chicken foetus into the air. The couple giggled at the way I jumped, and so did most of their friends.

'It's lucky,' the priest told me. 'Don't worry.'

'Permiso,' I said, and slipped past the congregation, who mostly nodded and waved before looking back to the fire and the prayers.

To get into the church, I had to step over pools of smoking red wax from the candles clustered by the door. The chapel smelled of roses soaked in vodka. Looking towards the altar told me why – another couple, two tall, strong-looking girls with dyed blond hair, standing before the altar, blessing themselves, spitting jets of liquor onto the bouquets piled under Maximón's feet. The statue here was bigger, taller, seated on a red throne, dressed in military fatigues, his face pained, like he was following regrettable orders. A crack ran down the centre of the face, but you could barely see it, it was a suture of glue that wavered into view when the candles flickered. His mouth was half open. The hollow inside was dark.

Tea-lights in rainbow colours guttered out in the metal troughs. The rafters were black with smoke, like a shipwreck seen through water, and the walls were busy with tiny stories – a man holding an iguana in his arms, train-tracks and lush green nowhere behind him, a prayer for his safe trip for him and Diana, the iguana, written by his mother on a Taz sticker in the corner of the picture; a Western Union remittance sent from the Port Authority bus-station by the same guy a few months later; bright etchings on tin showing Maximón descending from the clouds to save people from stabbings, drownings, robberies, rapes; photo after photo, year after year, of the same neon-lit strip-club, as if the owners were renewing their insurance policy.

Walking towards the back exit, I passed a glass case that held a head of Jesus, his scalp shaven, his cheeks scratched up, a scared look on his face, and I stumbled past it, heaving, through the back door and into the glare.

Out back were raised tombs painted in toothache shades of green, orange, lilac, blue, like the people had been wrapped up as little snacks for God. My head was really banging now, as I made my way over humps of dried clay and gravel, the crickets' noise a full-on shriek that beat in time with the ache in my head, becoming louder and louder until I had to sit down on a cracked pink tomb and wait for my breath to slow back to normal. A face stared out at me from below the cross on the tomb. The photo was brownish, with flares of yellow on it where rain had leaked through the cracks in the glass frame and run the phosphates. The dead kid had on these big metal Gerry Adams glasses, and there was a firm set to his chin that made him look a lot tougher than the scratchy beard and curly, soft-looking hair would have done on their own. The death-date read October 30th, 1986, and he'd been twenty-two when they'd gotten him. Across the path was another tomb with the same date marked on it, this one belonging to a seventeen-year-old girl. Beyond her, another student-age face looked out at the sun from another photo, the same date etched in the turquoise paint of the tomb. On the far side of the tomb I sat on, four brothers and sisters had been buried together, all of them in their late teens or early twenties, all of them dead on October 30th, 1986, all of them lying in a crypt donated by their university.

Crows spiralled, cawing, above the scrub and the cacti and the dead bodies and me. Over by the fence, a three-legged dog was trying to swallow something rotten. Every bite made her retch, cough, utter these weird, mucky-sounding snarls, but she kept going anyway. A dried clump of knotweed rustled past, startled her. She watched it pass, then looked over at me, giving me that black, rubbery non-grin that all dogs have.

Crossing into Honduras was easy. All I had to do was pretend I'd lost my visa, try to look the right amount of upset. The customs official glanced from me to my jeep.

'Mind if I have a look?'

'By all means,' I said, and escorted him over.

The inside made him frown.

'Have you got a firearm?' he said. 'Or any other contra-band? Because you can declare it now, if you want.' He held up his little notebook. 'I just add a zero to this fine right here, and nothing will happen.'

'You know who I am, don't you?' I said, trying to put that relaxed floating bravado into my voice like Puccini used to have.

The customs official held up my passport, smirking a little.

'What, I'm meant to recognise this name or something?'

'No, but you've heard of Puccini, haven't you?' I lit my cigarette with the dinged Zippo.

The customs official took a step back.

'That fucking carpenter is finished now,' I said, blowing smoke out the side of my mouth, just like Puccini used to. 'And I'm here instead. Alright?'

The customs official handed me back my passport, nodding.

'Understood, sir,' he said, and tore off the sheet from the top of the notepad with my name on it.

'What days do you work?' I said, and popped open the licence plate with my foot.

'Six days out of seven,' he said. 'Every other week.'

'Good.' I got out a wad of quetzales. 'Here's a little tip. I'll be seeing you.'

He goggled at me.

'What?'

'Well, it's just – what do we call you?' he said. 'If it isn't an indiscretion. I mean, I might need to tell other people. You know?'

'Morsa,' I said, and got into the car.

He was still standing there, the elastic-wrapped notes in his hand, as I drove across the border into Honduras, and then the dust flung up by my wheels swallowed the view of the border station in my wing mirrors.

When it got too dark to drive, I stayed at a hotel that had once been a house belonging to some Confederate slave-owners who'd fled after the Civil War, all tea-dark planks and balustrade pegs draped with Spanish moss. There was no hiding the blood in any of the money here. The next morning, I hit the Garifuna coast road, bending and swinging above cliffs that flickered silver with caught crisp-packets.

Kids were legging it out of the school gates when I reached the edge of the town Puccini had told me about. A man in shorts, a string vest, and a hat made of dried palm-fronds went wheeling his bike along the roadside. When I pulled in to ask him if he knew where Walter lived, he popped back the brim of his hat and leaned on my roof, checking me over. The sweat made his hair look like little grey peppercorns. Then he nodded, like I'd passed some kind of test, and sent me to a pulpería further up the road, where I found a grey-haired woman slapping wet clothes against a stone washboard on the porch of the shop. She stopped as I approached.

'You're the guy, right?' she said. 'Looking for Walter? Give me a moment.' She disappeared into the shop and emerged with a pot wrapped in a towel. 'He forgets to eat, even on his days off.' Then she pointed to where the road curved out of the scrubland and date-palms, towards a beach fronted with whitewashed houses. 'Third one on the left. He'll be the man in the hammock. Probably with a book.'

247

Walter was a tall man of about thirty-five. His hammock was a green net, strung from the posts of a porch that opened onto the beach. When he heard my jeep coming, he laid his book face-down on the terrace tiles and swung his legs out of the hammock. His shins were pocked all over with small round scars and scored with long thin ones.

Yawning, he stretched, scratched his braids, and got to his feet, then made a celebratory fist of one hand when he saw me taking the pot from the passenger seat.

'Cleotilda, man,' he said. 'Best mother-in-law ever.' He laid the pot on a small table beside the hammock. 'You here about the place?'

'That I am,' I said.

'Alright.' Walter took a set of keys out of his pocket. 'There's everything, you know, food, Wi-Fi, water, everything like that. You want me to show you around?'

'Maybe tomorrow.' I took the keys and clipped them to the end of Fidel Castro's foot.

'It's not bad.' Walter sank back into the hammock. 'Matter of fact, it's so good I moved back here.'

'From the States?'

He laughed. 'Yeah. Same as everyone around here.'

'You get the train?' I pointed at the marks on his shin.

He scratched under his chin. 'Who are you, man, a cop?'

'Quite the opposite.'

That got him laughing again. 'Well, alright. I'll show you around tomorrow.'

'There much to do?'

'Just when there's tourists. And that's, what? One week a year?'

'Perfect,' I said, and took my bag from the boot.

'Cool, man.' He gave me the peace sign, then took his Lydia Cacho book from the tiles. 'Well, have a nice rest now, you hear?'

'Don't forget to eat,' I said, and opened the door of the new place.

The fan was turning in the hall, over a sitting room that could have been the apartment I'd had back in Mexico City – same number of potted plants nodding in the draught, same knockoff '70s furniture. The floorboards had the dark creosote tang of those fuses Puccini had used to wrap up the bombs. Tall windows looked out on a surf that had the shine of melted turquoise, and the sand was white with splinters of coral. Palms tossed in the sea's big, slow breathing.

Another fan turned in the bedroom, lifting and dropping the mosquito-nets above the bed. After swallowing a glass of iced water from the jug on the bedside table, I took the little baggie of see-through bugs from my pocket, found the one that matched the serial number on the transmitter I'd given Maya, and stuck it to the wall behind the bed. Then I took Carlos' ashes out and plumped them down on the pillow beside mine, on top of the folded copy of *Proceso* with his face on the cover. After that I turned on my phone, lay down, typed in your number.

When I go back through everything, I stop the memory here, and I do it all differently. I press 'Dial'. You pick up. I say sorry for everything, even the stuff I don't even remember being my fault. You're OK with all of it.

But I didn't do any of that. All I did was look at the screen, listen to the pipes fill and empty, listen to the tide crash, listen to the blood in my veins and the breath in my lungs rush back in and out of me. Every inch of me felt too heavy to budge a single word out of me.

If I could have pressed fast-forward on the whole thing, zipped myself forward to the day when I could speak to you again, you know I would.

But right then, all I could do was press backspace on the number, and let myself fall asleep, because it's like I told Maya – the white guy never dies at the end of these things.

READ A CHAPTER FROM
TIM MACGABHANN'S *CALL HIM MINE*

'Tough and uncompromising:
you'll be glad you read it'
LEE CHILD

'A gripping off-the-wall
crime story. I loved it'
ADRIAN MCKINTY

'Intoxicating'
OBSERVER

'Exciting'
TELEGRAPH

'Feverish'
INDEPENDENT

'Arresting'
IRISH
INDEPENDENT

CALL

HIM

MINE

TIM ★ MACGABHANN

I

Nobody asked us to look. Every day, ever since, I still wish
we hadn't.

'Just a second,' Carlos said from behind me, crouched above
the body we'd found. His camera clicked so fast it could have
been the crickets shirring in the humid pre-dawn gloom.

'C'mon, man, your seconds last about ten minutes,' I said
through a yawn, wiping my glasses on my shirt, my voice a
rasp because four days of jeep and hotel-room air-conditioning
had given me a throat like a sock full of broken glass.

Carlos laughed and said, 'Yup.'

Until we found the body, I didn't expect to remember
a thing about Poza Rica. Just another story, we'd thought.
'*Waiting for the Black Gold Rush*' was the provisional headline
– a profile of Poza Rica, the crumbling oil city in Veracruz,
eastern Mexico, '*a place caught,*' I'd written, '*as though in sus-
pended animation, waiting for foreign investment to capitalise on the
region's fifteen billion barrels of oil – and raise the city to its former
height.*'

Just four days' worth of interviews, we'd figured, and we'd

be back home to file text and photos for the kind of dull, well-paid gig all freelancers dream of until they actually have to do one.

Yeah, well, you know. After eight years of living in Mexico, I should have known there's no such thing as just another story.

Call it Iguala or Reynosa, call it Manzanillo or Apatzingán, it's the same poor-town generica of pulled-down shutters and bad-luck motor shops, the same blue Alcoholics Anonymous triangles, the lurid blood cursive of gang tags.

It's the same taxi-rank shrines to Saint Jude and the Virgin of Guadalupe, the same faded Revolution murals, plaza, bandstand, and busts of the illustrious dead.

It's the same 'missing' posters on every lamppost and shop front, the same blood-and-sulphur odour of wrecked drains.

After we found the body, though, nothing would ever look the same again.

Ten minutes into our drive home to Mexico City, the AM radio playing bolero songs, we would stop now and again for photos of wellheads for the story: at the centre circle of a balding football field, in the yard of a pay-by-the-hour parking lot, at the bottom of an alley between the Best Western Hotel and the Banco Azteca.

So there we were, coasting down the main boulevard, closing in on five a.m., nobody heading out to work, nobody coming home from the late shift, the shadows under the big overpass holding only trash from the previous day's market, when we passed a small oil-derrick swinging back and forth at the bottom of an alley between a shuttered bar and a gleaming

Oxxo convenience store, and Carlos said, 'Oh, shit. Stop the jeep, *vato*.'

'What?' I'd said, parking at the top of the alley, but Carlos was already legging it towards someone lying on the ground.

For a second I wanted to tell him it was just a drunk, but then I got out of the jeep and saw the guy, his limbs splayed at angles no drunk sleeper would ever choose, and I stood there, winded, at the top of the alley, my heartbeat shaking my throat, my knuckles white where I gripped the jeep's doorframe, as a light, clammy rain petered down over me.

Bodies, I was OK around. They tell you the same amount of nothing, whether they sit calcified in a burned-out car, lie hog-tied and dumped on beaches, or rise greenish and soapy-looking from mass graves. But the poor guy lying by the oil derrick under the streetlight, his wasn't like any body I'd ever seen before. His counterfeit Levi's and white briefs had been pulled down to show a nest of pubic hair around a bloody hole, his cock and balls, peeled like grapes, left resting on his broken hands. His cheap pleather jacket was open over a polo shirt whose red wasn't dye, a red whose sugary butcher's-shop cloy drew the 7/11 coffee I'd been drinking in the jeep almost all the way back into my mouth.

'Don't get sick, *vato*,' said Carlos, laughing when he heard me spit. 'You'll wreck my shot.'

'Yes, because it's just gorgeous right now,' I said, lighting a cigarette to kill that dead kid's smell while the oil derrick just kept right on clanking.

People who tell you death has a smell, they're wrong: it's got dozens, and I only know some. After the Acapulco jet-ski drive-by me and Carlos had covered a couple years before, you couldn't tell the blood-smell from the bladderwrack parching on the shore. After the big warehouse massacre we'd reported on in Tlatlaya, in mid-2014, the main stink had come from the wheaten note of bullet-holed guts. At the mass graves uncovered in Taxco, the stench had been deep, fungal, butanoic, enough to put me off Roquefort forever.

Even from there, I could see what they'd done to the kid. The blood on his shirt wasn't from a bullet-wound: his neck was a collar of bruises where he'd had the life choked out of him, and there were no punctures in his chest or face. Matter of fact, he had no face. That's where all the blood had come from: his face had been taken, his eyes thumbed out, leaving a wet red mask specked with dust and grit, his teeth climbed black. A Stanley knife, I figured: criss-crossed incisions edged the wound above his right jaw, and, from the ragged edge of skin under his left, I could tell they'd stopped cutting once they'd worked up enough of a loose end to tear the rest of his face off with their hands.

An ant picked over the ridge of bone and cartilage where his nose had been. My stomach gurgled like a volcano. Carlos stooped to blow away the ant, then unlidded his camera.

'Watch the street,' said Carlos gently, his back turned to me.

What I wanted to say was, *If you don't hurry, I'll be sick everywhere.*

What I said was, 'Ugh, fine,' and swallowed back the sour taste in my mouth.

'You're OK, *vato*,' Carlos said to the body as he knelt with his hand above the kid's mussed and bloody hair, murmuring so quietly he could have been praying. 'It's over now.'

Carlos used to say ghosts lingered at murder scenes for a little while after the victim died. Used to say it was something the Jesuits taught him at the high school back in Juárez. Used to say that because of how furiously the soul was expelled from its body, the soul was too scared, too shocked to fray out into nowhere.

'Don't be scared,' he said to the faceless kid, taking a long drag of cigarette smoke to breathe over the body like funeral incense. 'Don't let us keep you.' He raised the camera lens to start taking his photos. The flash was the white of candlelight. 'We won't take a minute.'

'It was "I won't take a second" a minute ago,' I said.

'Take it easy,' said Carlos, and I couldn't tell if it was me or the kid he was talking to.

'We were headed home,' I said. 'I can't believe you.'

'Relax,' said Carlos. 'We're having fun, aren't we?'

The street beyond the alleyway was dead as a moon. There weren't even the usual sharp-faced teenagers in brand-new baseball caps and space-boot-looking trainers guarding corners, their smartphones and pistols hidden in their kangaroo-pouch bags. They'd been everywhere the whole four days we'd been in Poza Rica: hanging around alleys, lingering by market stalls, even tipping off cops outside houses in poor neighbourhoods.

But now? Nobody. Just the boulevard's matte and tarnished buildings, just streetlamps mottled with old petrol fumes.

'C'mon, man,' I said, watching a wounded dog clitter past on its three good legs. 'How many pictures do you need?'

'Just keep an eye out, yeah?' His boots gritted as he shifted for the right angle.

You can spend a lifetime watching over people. All through secondary school, back in Ireland, I'd been the guy who'd keep an eye out for teachers during lunchtime scuffles, or hidden the booze nicked from the drinks cabinets of other lads' parents, or stowed my mates' weed and ecstasy stashes in my flat, and now here I was keeping sketch while someone else took a picture he really shouldn't.

'Is your back turned?' said Carlos behind me. 'I'm almost done.'

From the red hills of Michoacán to the flicker-lit Zeta nightclubs in Coatzacoalcos; from the mass graves in the stiff-grassed hills of Cocula to the Huejutla warehouses where rats and damp gnawed the Gulf cartel's unlaundered bales of money; from the Kodachrome skies and parched dirt roads of the Tarahumara Mountains – to here, to now, to this alley of broken glass and drying blood in Poza Rica, Veracruz – in every one of those places, I'd watched over Carlos while he got his photos, and I hadn't fucked up, not even once.

'Bro,' I said, turning over my shoulder to see Carlos' face lowered to a face that wasn't a face any more.

Carlos' hand was inside the dead kid's jacket, reaching for the inside pocket.

'You'll get your prints everywhere,' I said.

'Oh, yeah, because forensics are, like, super-diligent round here,' Carlos said, the kid's wallet already flipped open in his hand.

'I can't believe this,' I said, even though I could.

Carlos opened the kid's wallet and slid a Universidad Vera-cruzana student card out from behind the Cinepolis and KFC discount cards, then took a photo of the ID. Name: Julián Gallardo. Date of Birth: October 1996.

'*Mire, güey*,' said Carlos, sliding the card back into the wallet and the wallet back into Julián's pocket. 'No harm, no foul.'

Tyres squalled beyond where I'd seen the dog jogging out of sight.

'You weren't keeping an eye out.' Carlos laid his camera on the ground.

Gravel crunched. A siren cut through my skull. Then police-car lights washed over us, red and blue and halogen white, and doors slammed as two shadows climbed from the big white Guardia Civil pickup, while a third aimed a mounted AR-15 assault rifle down at us.

'Get down,' said one cop, in a frightened whisper.

'Can't believe you fucked this up,' Carlos said.

'All right, man, whatever you say,' I said to Carlos, and got to my knees, hands behind my head, my press laminate held high and its lanyard around my wrist.

The first cop moved forward, the second one covering him from behind, light gleaming along the telephone-wire coils of his gun's security cord.

So we knelt there in the white glare, hands behind our heads, broken glass pricking through the knees of our jeans, the cops' shadows looming bigger, their footsteps closing in.

2

The two cops stepped out of the light and into our faces. The first to reach us took the laminate from my hand, while the cop standing in the back of the pickup swivelled his mounted rifle back and forth along the avenue. You could still hear the clunk of the derrick and my jeep radio petering sad melodies into the dark.

'This is a crime scene,' said the first cop.

My skin wasn't skin any more: just a hot prickling shiver all over.

'We thought he was alive,' I said.

The cop looked over at Julián, then back at me.

A wad of shit pressed hot against my asshole.

'Until we got close,' I said.

The cop didn't say anything, just gave Carlos a chin-jut.

'You took pictures?' he said.

'Was about to,' said Carlos. 'Sorry.'

The first cop smashed Carlos across the jaw with the stock of his pistol and said, 'You stupid bastard. You'll get us all killed.'

The word *Help* hit the roof of my mouth and bounced back into silence, but Carlos didn't even cry out, just went down, docile as a felled cow. The second cop kept the muzzle of his gun trained on him.

'Get his ID,' the first cop told the second one.

Moments like that, nothing matters to you. Your head's got the clean emptiness of a spilled-out goldfish bowl. Nothing you thought mattered means a thing, not your coffee-breath or your headache, not the shit-wad about to hit your thighs, not even your memories of the people you won't see again. All you are is the tarmac smell in your nose and the grit and broken glass under your hands.

The cop loomed over me, and said: 'You want to end up like this kid?'

'No,' I said. My breath skittered loose grit.

'Me neither,' said Carlos.

The cop crouched beside me. 'You know who this town belongs to?'

'We're doing a story about oil,' I said. 'Just numbers. Nothing about crime. Heading home, we saw a body, stopped to see what was up.' I sucked in air that tasted of road. 'That's all.'

The first cop pressed his fingers to his forehead. 'Look, I'll repeat myself. Do you *know* who this town belongs to?'

'I don't think they know,' said the second cop. This guy, his voice was high, nasal, a newbie's. 'They wouldn't be here if they did.'

The first cop looked at me, then at Carlos, then at the newbie cop.

'Let's get out of here, seriously,' said the newbie cop, a plea in his voice now.

The first cop dropped his eyes to the ground, nodded, then holstered his gun.

'You've been lucky tonight,' he said, his hands on his hips. He shook his head.

Carlos slipped me a wink from further along the alley floor. His jaw was red, darkening to cinnamon, and his lip trailed a string of dark blood. The salt taste welling up under his tongue; I tasted that under mine as well.

The second cop said, 'I'm sorry about your jaw.'

The first cop jerked his head towards our jeep and said, 'What are you waiting for? Go, *go*.'

Carlos dusted off the knees of his jeans, patted my shoulder. 'Come on, yeah?'

The second cop coughed and the air was instantly the smell of puke.

'Where are they getting these new guys?' said Carlos, his arm around me.

'Ten years of this drug-war shite.' I held my press laminate up at the third cop in the back of the pickup. 'Not many tough lads left.'

'Must be that,' said Carlos, and looked back over his shoulder at the body in the white-lit alley. 'Poor guy, though. Wonder where they're taking him.'

The cop who'd hit Carlos dragged Julián Gallardo by his shoulders towards the pickup. The one who'd talked to me was muttering into a radio now. With one hand he held one of Julián's feet. The other foot dragged.

'Same place they all go,' I said, and turned the key in the ignition.

The cops slung Julián into the back of the pickup, and he thunked against the metal, his limbs awry, and the cop on the radio kicked away the lines his heels had dragged through the dirt and grit.

'Yeah,' said Carlos. 'Nowhere.'

Acknowledgements

Love and gratitude to Jany, Ma, Da, Beck, Tom, Marianne, Kate, Ger, Marée, Richie, Paul and the whole Keenan Clan, David, John, Richie, Kevin, Clare, Deirdre, Maura, Frank and the whole Smyth Clan, Ruki, Pichus, Lucha (La Musa), Tere, Moncho, Manuel, Manolito, Mariana, Diana, Rafael, Rafita, Santi, Abraham, Liz, Fer, Diegui, Amy Stillman, Julian Duane, Duncan Tucker, Carlos Ortega, Diego Gerard, Zakia Uddin, James Barnes, Ronan Fitzgerald, Dave Graham, David Lida, Jan-Albert Hootsen, C.M. Lindley, Frank Goldman, Maxine Patroni, Magda Bogin, Mica Sánchez, Laura Garibay, Rosa Lyster, Mark O'Connell, Paul Murray, Eddie P., Oisín Murphy-Hall, Lucía Gaxiola Hinojosa, Mia Gallagher, Ian Rankin, Philly Malicka, María Portilla, Adrian McKinty, Iona McLaren, Nicole Flattery, Paul Boyle, Tadhg Coakley, Adam Foulds, Ayşegül Savaş, Lizzie Hutchings, Ámbar Barrera, Gina Balibrera, Lee Child, Levi Vonk, Gabriela Damián, Daniel Escoto, Paco Cantú, Dylan Brennan, Liliana Pérez, Salman Rushdie, Rachel Eliza Griffiths, Pergentino José Ruiz, Drew Nutter, Marjorie

Brennan, Alice Jacquier, Shelley Hastings, Brian McGilloway, Steve Cavanagh, Maxim Jakubowski, Luis Orozco, Azam Ahmed, Grant Cogswell, Jonathan Levinson, Josh Partlow, Kevin Sieff, Robbie Whelan, Keith Dannemiller, Bénédicte Desrus, Nathaniel Janowitz, Joe Greenwood, Tommy Karshan, Andrew Cowan, Dudley Althaus, Steve Woodman, Karl McDonald, Cathal Wogan, Tommy Murtagh, Emma Flynn, David Hartery, Mags and Neil Gunning, Elaine Egan, Colin Barrett, Paul Whyte, John Patrick McHugh, Oisín Fagan, Johnny Shaw, Óscar de Muriel, Sam Hurcom, Sean McTiernan, Chris McGeorge, David K. Wayne, Isabel Ashdown, Brendan Barrington, Danny Denton, Declan Meade, Austin Cullen, Emily Ghadimi, Kevin Barry, Wendy Erskine, Kyle Rapps, Michael Howey, Bill Cox, Neil Broadfoot, Luke Kennard, Sarah Fletcher, John Reid, Duncan Falconer, Karl Meakin, Róisín Agnew, Hannah Partis-Jennings, Kunzes Goba, Shaun Rolph, Jay Stringer, Chris McQueer, Robin Myers, the quite frankly magical Federico Andornino and Sam Copeland, Katie Espiner, Tom Noble, Emad Akhtar, Cait Davies, Ellie Freedman, Alainna Hadjigeorgiou, Alex Layt, Kim Bishop, Clarissa Sutherland and the whole gang at W&N and Orion, to the Arts Council of Ireland for their generous financial assistance, to the Under the Volcano 2020 crew, to Anais Taracena's brilliant *El silencio del topo*, to the Friends of Dr Bob, to Irene and Vero from the fonda, to Daniel from the Krispy Kreme on Calle Gelati, to Legends Club.

A special thank you to all the readers of *Call Him Mine* and *How to Be Nowhere* – I'm so amazed and even more grateful that you exist.

And boundless love and gratitude to Jany again – first, last, always.